REDKOIN

Jeremy Croston

Bolt Publishing, LLC

An Orlando based publishing company

ISBN Number: **979-8679301320**

Printed in the United States

1 9 2 8 3 7 4 6 5

Publisher Note:

This book is a work of fiction.
All of the names, places,
and events that occur are from
the author's imagination.
Any resemblance to an actual
person, alive or dead, place,
historical event, or business establishment
is purely coincidental.

Contributions:

Editorial Team:
Lead Editor – Karen Croston
Content and Story – Stephanie Croston

Cover Design – Jeremy Croston
Social Media and Web Design – Ryan Latterell

What are YOU investing in?

Welcome to the ruthless and sketchy world of investing. When IPO's flop and new cryptocurrencies hitting the open market, you need to know what you are investing in. Could it be the next vaccine to save the world… or could it be something much more sinister?

Come along on a thrilling ride as Kyle Carlisle discovers what's really fueling this new wave of investments and just how it truly impacts his life.

Praise for Jeremy Croston:

"Once I started reading Jeremy Croston's City of Chaos I immediately thought of the classic, old-time superhero stories – the pulp fiction comic books, per se. The collectibles in the stores, 10 cent comic reads, with the storyboards, super-heroes and villains, with their animated violence and damsels in distress. Croston's fictional world plays like the comic worlds of Marvel and DC, but Croston uses more of a personal and interesting touch with new and relatable characters."

-A.L. Mengel, City of Chaos

"Every fight scene or altercation is perfectly drawn out, with the protagonist's strengths and weaknesses on full display. I found myself sitting on the edge of my seat with every alteration wondering if and how the protagonist was going to escape."

-Braskyyy, Malice of the Cross

More from the Author:

***Drakovia**:*
Malice of the Cross
Rise of the Seventh Reich

The Negative Man Saga:
City of Chaos
Stormfall
Prelude to Chaos
Legends Can Die
Twilight Days

Twilight of the Gods:
The Wolves of Valhalla
Rise of the Serpent

TheCrostonverse
Bull River Blues
RedKoin
Hammerhead Bay (Winter 2021)

Dedication

To Patricia Hopfauf; you may be gone but your spirit lives on through all of us.

Table of Contents

April 14th, 2016; Sherwood, CA

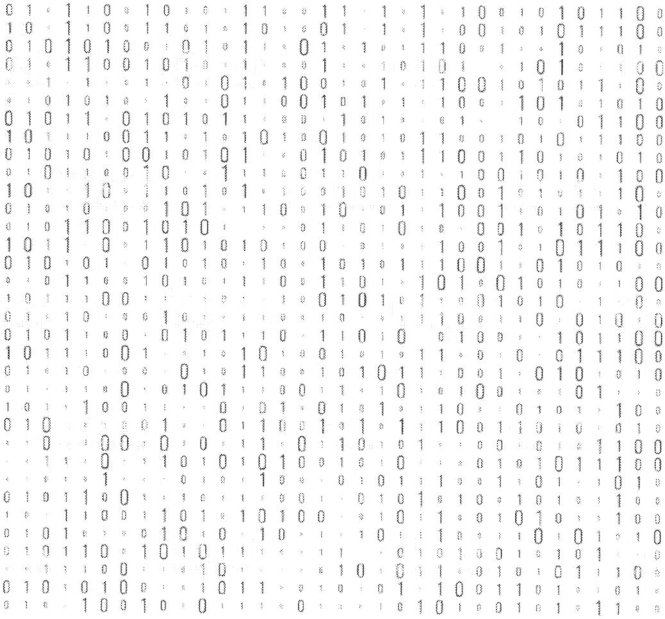

1

Collateral

Something pledged as security for repayment of a loan, to be forfeited in the event of a default.

All of this blasted trouble over corporate espionage.

Or more accurately, the price of stupid, no good stocks.

This is what happens what you get a bunch of nerds from two biotech firms squabbling over secrets. Agent Rebeca Schulte and I were directly in the middle of a pissing contest between GenX and War Dog Labs. GenX claimed that War Dog stole from them. What Schulte and I uncovered in our investigation proved not only that the claims were true, but even more sinister actions were afoot. That's the only reason the two of us were here tonight.

Gunshots fired over my head. This was pretty damn annoying. "Schulte," I yelled, "do you see where the bullets are coming from?"

"I think the second and third windows, from the third floor as you thought," she answered. "What should we do?"

Our impromptu raid on War Dog Labs wasn't going well at all. It was bad enough that every step tonight, whoever was orchestrating this was one step ahead of us. Now, we were pinned down and my stomach growled, wanting to finish that slice of pie from the café.

This pissed me off.

"Schulte, cover me and get us back up," I growled over the shots.

She stood up quickly and began pumping her Glock .40 towards where we thought our assailants were. Backup wouldn't be here for five to six minutes at the earliest; plenty of time for these bastards to burn any evidence I needed. The distraction worked. I had maybe a few seconds to race through the cars and into the doors of the office building. I took a deep breath, regretting all the cigarettes I'd smoked over the years and went for it.

Lady Luck was finally on my side tonight. I lowered my shoulder and broke down the doors. Once inside, no one was shooting at me. Schulte was still taking heavy fire, so I needed to get to these jerks and fast. The building only had three floors; my gut told me they were on the third. I took the stairs, knowing the elevator would probably be pretty heavily guarded once the doors opened on the floor. I took them two at a time, huffing and puffing along the way.

When I got to the top floor landing, I took a second to catch my breath.

Don't smoke, kids.

I slowly turned the handle and swung the door open. Bingo, two gunners with their rifles pointed out the window, firing at my partner. Not today. Two shots were all that I needed to put these guys down. They wouldn't be shooting anyone ever again.

By the time I'd gotten back to the first floor, Schulte was inside the building. "This place already looks cleaned out."

I did a quick look around. “Shit, don’t tell me we’re too late.”

“Let’s go floor by floor, Muldoon.”

Schulte took the west side while I meandered eastward. Most of the cubicles on my side were cleared out, nothing more than maybe a stray pen or paperclip lying around. It was becoming more and more obvious that we’d gotten here too late. Still, the fact there were shooters here to greet us was a telling sign. First, they knew we were getting close. Second, why would anyone be here for us if there still wasn’t a secret or two to learn?

“Muldoon, come check this out.”

I wasn’t having any luck with my side. “What’d you find, Schulte?” I asked.

She held up a balance sheet, or part of one by the looks of it. “Have you ever heard of Ares Commerce? Seems they may have been financing something here.”

As she passed it over, I began reading what little information was there. “What are these? Chemicals?”

“Those are ticker symbols, Muldoon. It looks like this place was being funded through a hedge fund. That’d make sense, considering the valuation this place had just a few months ago,” she explained.

“How do you know so much about this crap?”

"I interned at Chuck-Trade for a few summers in college."

"Does it give us anything useful?"

"Besides a money trail, you were half-right. Most of these symbols listed here are for companies that produce chemicals. Good eye," she teased me.

I handed it back; it meant more to her than it did to me. I rummaged through the next desk, finding more papers that were full of numbers and equations that meant nothing to me. I wanted something tangible. I tossed the rest of the stuff to the side in annoyance.

It didn't take long to finish sweeping the first floor before we were on the second. I knew the third floor was executive office space, so I was glad to see some actual lab equipment and supplies on this floor. I was beginning to wonder just how in the hell this place actually produced anything tangible. A lot of the supplies had been broken and destroyed. This was to be expected; what a seasoned investigator like myself was looking for was sloppy work. When people were up against the wall, pressed for time, they didn't clean up so well.

My hunch was right.

There was a waste can filled with crumpled up paper. Someone had probably meant to burn this, but yeah, ran out of time. I picked up the can and dumped the contents out on the nearest desk. If I thought the stock balance sheet was confusing, the writing on these papers was even more so. The first one talked about something called the Aphrodite Paradox and how the red coins would be the answer. What the bloody hell did that mean?

"Everything okay, Muldoon?"

"Jibberish, just nothing but mad writings and bull crap."

Schulte picked it up and began reading it herself. "I wish I understood this, Muldoon, but even my elite college education doesn't help."

Ugh, she enjoyed the little digs here and there. I may not have gone to some fancy California university, but years of hard-earned experience was all the education I needed. And those years of education told me that these people were on drugs or just downright crazy to begin with. Maybe they left this basket just to confuse us, disorient us with weird conjecture. The second balled up document had even more nonsense, random words like plague, ruination, and storm. Storm was circled a great many times as if it was more important than the rest. Annoyed, I grabbed an evidence bag and began placing everything inside.

"This says Pandemos," Schulte said, breaking my concentration.

"Just put whatever into evidence. Maybe some of the shrinks back at the field office can figure this out."

"No," she said. "I have a name. Not a name I recognize though, but it's clear as day on this scrap."

She held it up for me to see. "Kyle Carlisle? Who the hell is that?"

I'm going to level with all of you right now. All FBI agents have apps on their phones that allow them to search for a person by name and give them everything that the federal government has on them with the swipe of a finger. I pulled out my xPhone and quickly found six individuals named Kyle Carlisle in the database. However, only one was local.

Bingo.

"This must be the in. He's some sort of stock broker for a firm called Global Options."

"I doubt that," Schulte countered. "Global Options is one of the newest firms to pop up. A hedge fund would be doing business with one of the big boys."

Before I could probe more into her knowledge, more bullets began to fly. I tackled Schulte to the floor as we were under fire again. "I thought you said backup was five minutes away," I growled. "It's been at least twenty already!"

"I didn't see you radio anyone, either."

We each checked our weapons. "I have half a clip left."

"I only have four bullets left."

That made sense she had less rounds than I did, given that she'd covered me earlier. I was about to stand up and return some fire when a very calm female voice issued a command, "Stop."

Just like that, everything stopped. As we stood up, a middle-aged businesswoman was standing at the elevator door, flanked by agents Taft and Cleveland. There was a very blank look in their eyes, like they were hypnotized. It was the same look that Megan and Rowbick had earlier. They were the ones who were firing at us!

"Just who in the hell do you think you are?"

"My name is Venus Typhon, head of War Dog Labs. Thanks to your brilliant investigative work, Agent Drew Muldoon, I have to shut this down and begin anew."

"Hey," Schulte snipped, "I did most of the leg work, Ms. Typhon."

"That you did, Agent Rebecca Schulte. I'll get to you in a minute, but first, allow me to get rid of the collateral."

Typhon snapped her fingers and agents Taft and Cleveland pointed their guns at each other and fired. In a matter of moments, the bureau was down two good men. It was horrible to watch Taft and Cleveland just shoot each other, no emotion in their eyes as they fired their guns. Both Schulte and I snapped our Glocks into place, ready to kill Typhon. Even as I tried to pull my trigger, something was stopping me from killing her.

"Sorry, my dears. Unfortunately, even if I did allow you to shoot me, it would do no good."

"What the hell is going on here?" I grunted, as I tried to pull the trigger.

"I am changing the world, Agent Muldoon. My plans are ever changing, ever growing. Time will tell, Agent Muldoon, time that you won't even remember after this encounter," she explained.

Her attention shifted to Schulte. "I don't need a monologue, ma'am," Schulte said dryly.

"For you, my dear, I don't need to bore you. I need to borrow you, actually."

Typhon walked right up to Schulte and placed her hand on Schulte's shoulder. "To sóma sou eínai dikó mou," she whispered.

It felt like a bomb went off on the second floor of War Dog Labs. I flew backwards, landing on top of a desk that crashed under the fall. Splinters of wood pierced through my coat and shirt, digging into my skin. As I laid there in pain, Schulte walked over, looking down at me - with disgust?

Oh no! This wasn't Schulte anymore.

"What did you do to her?"

"My previous host was beginning to fight back, Agent Muldoon. Until I am truly ready to reveal my true self to the world, host bodies will have to do," Pseudo-Schulte said.

Host bodies? True self? Son of a bitch; we were dealing with aliens! "Go back to your own planet, alien scum," I hissed.

"Aliens? That's quite the imagination. I just might let you keep that little tidbit before I wipe your memory of this incident."

"Why not kill me?"

"Every great event in world history needs a witness to walk away. And you're mine, Agent Muldoon."

There was nothing I could do. I was compromised and barely hanging on. As I looked up at the body of my partner, I made a silent vow to do everything in my power to free her from this… witch? Alien? Demon? I hadn't the foggiest idea what I was dealing with. She might be able to wipe my mind, I thought, but my hatred would lead me back.

"Good bye for now, Agent Muldoon," Typhon whispered. "I mními diagráfike."

And everything went black.

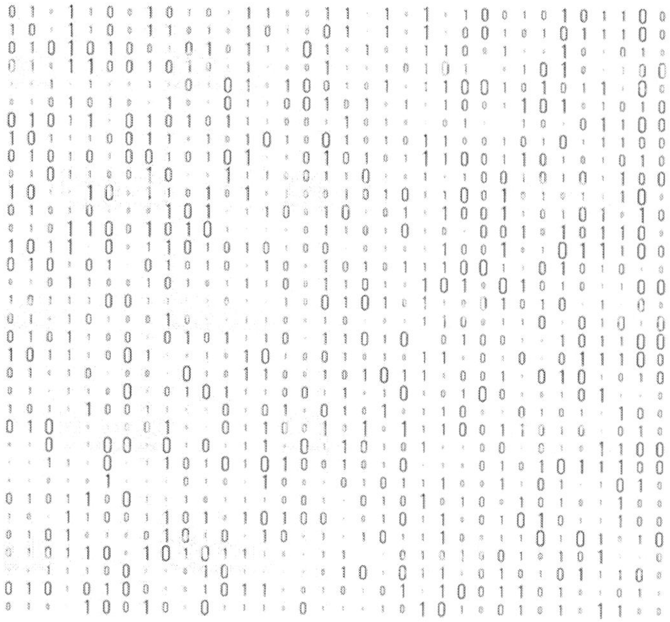

2

Day Trades

The buying and selling of securities on the same day, often online, on the basis of small, short-term price fluctuations.

"**Sherwood Financial, Kyle Carlisle** here," I answered for like the thirtieth time today.

"Kyle, it's Sam. Get me into five GenX calls and another ten K worth of RedKoin, my man," Sam Iam rambled obnoxiously into the phone.

Don't get me wrong, Sam was a good guy, but the way he gambled his family's cash on high risk option contracts and vanity crypto currency was the obnoxious part. And the most annoying thing about all of it was he was so damn good at it. Every time I thought he screwed himself over, he came out smelling like roses two days later.

Pissed me right off, sometimes.

"You got it, Sam."

The moment I hung up the phone, I did a double take on the order Sam had placed. Another buyer for GenX, a biotech firm whose initial public offering flopped a few months back. It was weird people were buying anything security position in that albatross. Still, my responsibility was to my client and, against my better instinct, placed the unsolicited order as I'd been directed. That was the crappy thing about my job; I had a duty to my clients but they could basically ignore everything I said and do whatever the hell they wanted.

After the trades were executed, I left my office and went to grab a cup of cold brew from the tap in the cafeteria. Only Sherwood Financial had such luxuries. The last place I worked for only had depression and demerits. They actually had the nerve to mark your permanent record if you called in sick. At least I was out of that place. Here, I had a lot more freedom and relief. I didn't go home each night to my apartment feeling like I wanted to stab my eyes out.

As I drank my caffeine kick, my boss, Jeremiah Thomas walked in. He was dressed in jeans and a Flyers hoodie. You would've never known by the looks of it, that the guy had more knowledge about the market than anyone I'd ever met. He was also a giant conspiracy theorist. He was the perfect guy to soundboard off about weird and shady trades.

"Sam called in this morning," I said.

Everyone knew Sam. "Oh God," Jeremiah moaned. "What idiotic thing did he do now?"

"He bought a bunch of RedKoin and options on GenX. The RedKoin I get, everyone's investing in that crypto, but GenX? Didn't the IPO fail miserably?"

Jeremiah tapped his chin. "As far as I heard, they bombed pretty epically. However, late last year, when that weird flu popped up for a few months, didn't they produce some sort of treatment for it?"

I didn't watch a lot of news as it was very depressing, but I did remember something about it. "Still, one bullet after a series of failures doesn't seem like the best investment, but hey, who am I to tell Sam what to do?"

Jeremiah leaned in. "Rumors on some of the sites I run with every so often claim that GenX created that strain of flu with the treatment already produced. You didn't hear that from me, though," he added.

I finished my cup of coffee and stood up. "Duty calls, sir. I'll catch up with you later."

The rest of my day was a lot of the same - order this, sell that, and why didn't my order execute? By four forty-five, I was pretty well good and done. I switched my phone to 'out of office' and began going down the rabbit hole of internet searches. What started as getting stats for the upcoming fantasy baseball draft turned into searching the rumor Jeremiah had told me. I knew it wasn't smart to do these searches on a computer that was monitored by the US Government, but they were only silly rumors. Nothing Jeremiah ever came up with was actually serious...

Until this one.

It took a few minutes, but I actually came across a site that had stories right from two employees that had worked at GenX. Two days after the story had been released on the blog, both employees were found dead in a one car accident. I wanted to chalk that up to a coincidence, but the next story was even crazier. An unknown whistleblower tried to take the story public only to be arrested the next day for drug trafficking. He apparently yelled at reporters as he was being dragged into the station that GenX was run by aliens.

"There's something inhuman happening behind those walls," was one of the ex-employee's direct quotes.

That part was obviously the ramblings of a mad man, but still, this was too much proof. Something weird was going on at GenX and whatever it was, it was lining their pockets with money from stock sales. Their profits had soared in the last quarter of the previous year and were projected to blow up even more in the first quarter this year.

I quickly cleared my history and closed my laptop. I didn't want to know anymore. It was already five thirty and most of the office had left. I grabbed my coat and my keys and left without so much as a word to anyone. I was pretty freaked out and this was all Jeremiah's fault. Damnit! Why did his crazy theory have to have some legs? As I pushed the start on the ignition, my Jeep came to life and I pulled out of the parking garage as fast as I could. Why was I so paranoid? I kept looking in my rearview mirror thinking someone was going to get me.

When I got back to my apartment, I locked the door before grabbing a cold beer and some leftover pizza. All I needed to do was put on the game, let the beer relax me, and eventually fall asleep. The plan started to work until about halftime of the game; with the score a complete blow-out; my mind began to drift. It drifted right back to GenX.

"C'mon, Kyle," I grumbled to myself. "Don't go down that rabbit hole."

But then the commercials began to drag, the announcers started talking about random facts no one cared about, and the game never got close again. Before I knew it, my tablet was in my hands and I was searching for more information on GenX. Most of the top results were press headlines or market reports that talked about a glowing future to the once dead IPO. The weird part about everything was no one spoke about where the influx of cash to pull off this miracle came from. Before I got into the brokerage side, I was an intern for an investment company and I knew a thing or two about struggling companies. The most basic, red-blooded American way to reverse a huge loss was to haggle new investors into opening their pockets.

And that's what bothered me most.

Where did the money come from?

It was a little after midnight when I got something small, but something telling. Two months prior to the record profits beginning, there was a report made to the state administrator talking about a private placement being made. A private placement was an offering to the filthy stinking rich (aka hedge funds) and venture capitalists. The only organization that was named on the report was one called Ares Commerce.

"Don't do this," I said again, only to myself.

I immediately looked up Ares Commerce to see who else they had invested in. Venture capitalists normally liked to dabble in all sorts of weird and exotic businesses with the hopes of huge returns. GenX Biotech was their only holding. There was no history before or after. Their website didn't even have a telephone number to reach out to investor services. There was no question about it, this was obviously a shell company and the funds came from illegal activity. The alien theory was fun, but it was time to put that to bed.

It was just another layering operation.

With that peace of mind, I could go to bed and not have to worry about this anymore.

****

The next morning was a lot more of the same. I was in the middle of telling some young punk that no, I didn't have to un-restrict his account for his stupid day trading practices. Day trading was the ridiculous habit of buying and selling a stock on the same day. Whatever happened to buying something and holding onto it for the long run? Long term gains, people! Well, in the middle of that delightful conversation, there was a knock on my door. Standing there was a well-dressed Asian woman, holding a briefcase. Her black hair was pulled back in a ponytail and her expression was very friendly. Everything from her glasses, to her dress and shoes told a story of being very expensive.

"Danny, as fun as this has been, your account is frozen for ninety days. Have a wonderful rest of your week."

"Are you that polite with all of your clients?" she asked as soon as I hung up.

I couldn't help but to laugh. "If you're going to be a dumb trader, then I'm going to treat you as such."

My new guest placed her briefcase on my small, wooden desk. She flipped it open and inside were stock certificates, a very rare sight. Each certificate was made out to Amy Pandemos. I began to assume that it was she who was in front of me. The other odd thing was that these were all GenX stock certificates. There had to be hundreds of thousands of dollars' worth of shares right there, in that briefcase.

"If you don't mind, I'd like to share my dilemma with you," she said very casually, as if what she'd shown me was nothing more than a cool meme on her phone. "As you can see, I am well vested in GenX. In fact, me and my holding company own just over thirty-five percent of the company. This represents about three percent; I'm looking for a firm and a broker I can trust. You came highly recommended, Kyle. I hope I'm making the right choice."

That was a bit of a surprise. "Who recommended me and this firm?"

"That investor wished to remain a silent partner in my doings. My goal is to begin keeping my certificates with capable custodians, in the event of something… happening."

"Absolutely, we can assist you with that," I responded, still a bit unnerved by this impromptu meeting.

"Let me be clear, you are the only agent I wish to deal with. If I have to deal with anyone else, I will remove these shares and find another firm to deal with. I am not trying to be difficult, but this is business and in business, you have to trust your agent."

"Can I be frank with you?"

"Of course, Kyle."

"I work at a firm where all of our trades are self-directed. I'm just a blip on the map in the brokerage world, so it's just a tad strange for someone of your stature to come to me and

Sherwood Financial for something like this. You want to trust me, then I need to trust you," I explained.

"My instincts were right; you are the man for this job," she answered. She still didn't give me a straight answer. "I'll be back in two days with a host of block trades that will need to be performed. Keep those shares safe and I will give you some answers."

She stood up and so I did the same. Shaking her hand, "I look forward to assisting you further, Ms. Pandemos."

"It's Miss Pandemos to everyone else, but you may call me Amy."

****

As soon as Amy left, I began Googling the shit out of her. Unfortunately, I didn't even get to the first result before A.B. Barber stormed into my office. "Who the hell was that hot chick, Kyle? And did I hear block trades?"

A.B. was a good dude. He was covered in tattoos and looked more like a pro wrestler named Turbo Destruction than an agent at a brokerage firm. But hell, A.B. knew his stuff inside and out. When I first got hired, he was the agent responsible for getting me up to snuff on option trading and crypto-currency. I would never be out of this guy's debt.

Chuckling, "That was one Amy Pandemos. Apparently, she's with some sort of holding company."

He just whistled in appreciation. In my mind, I was putting the dots together - Amy Pandemos had to be with Ares Commerce in some way. She had said holding company and I'd already discovered that Ares was a venture capital company. I needed to get back into the mystery.

Did I, actually?

"Earth to Kyle, you listening man?"

"Yeah sorry, long night. I was just spacing for a minute."

Fortunately, at that moment, the phones began to ring for both of us. A.B. grumbled something about not feeling it today and dragged himself back to his office. As I answered the phone, I was able to get back to the first link in my search. "Sherwood Financial, Kyle Carlisle," I answered robotically.

The guy on the other end began griping about a trade we busted and as he was throwing out profanity and insults. I started reading Amy Pandemos' profile. She'd been a rich socialite for the first twenty-two years of her life before she enrolled in UC-Berkeley, majoring in finance. She'd graduated in just two and half years. Not long after that, the trail went cold as Amy Pandemos' life became much more private without all the glitz and glamour that it had previously. There was no mention of Ares Commerce or any holding company. It was a complete mystery.

After my call, I delivered the certificates to the physical security department to have them recorded and locked away for safekeeping. Again, most people were just fine with the electronic records of share ownership. When I handed over the briefcase to Carl Consider, the head of physical shares, he nearly lost his mind. He had to count all the shares and their values two or three times before he signed off on them and placed them in the vault.

"The last time I saw this much paper, I think Bush was still running the country."

"Which one?" I joked.

He didn't take it that way. "The old man," he responded, confirming just how long he'd been in the business.

I'm not sure why I had this thought, but it came right out. "Carl, can you do something and keep it between the two of us?"

"Sure kid, what's up?"

"Can you change the combination to the vault? This many shares and the way they were delivered, I don't know, but my gut says we should err on the safe side."

He scratched his chin for a second. “Yeah, I don’t think that’ll be a problem at all.”

With that plan in place I went home, still a bit perplexed over the day’s events.

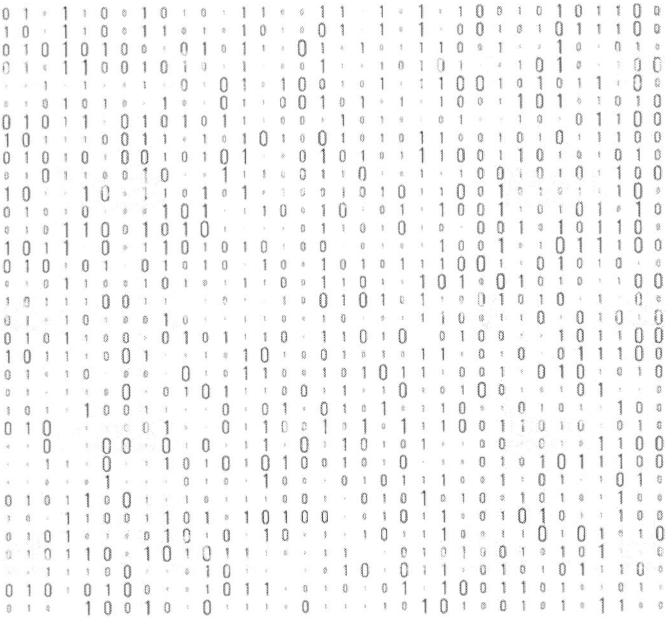

3

Selling Short

A trading strategy that speculates on the decline in a stock or other securities price.

"Why are the police here?" I asked myself as I pulled into work.

I was parked and out of my car as my manager, Jeremiah approached. "Someone tried to break into our vault last night, but luckily, nothing happened. Apparently, Carl changed the combination last night and whoever it was, couldn't break it."

Thank goodness he listened to me. The last thing we needed was breaking news of how we lost a bunch of stock certificates one day after we took custody of them. Plus, I needed to gain Amy's trust so I could learn more about her holding company. If there was inside trading, money laundering, or a host of other illegal activities happening, I had a duty as a registered representative to learn about it and report it to the financial crimes network. And the only way I could do that was by proving I was a good agent.

As I was standing there, a rather gruff looking guy with messy brown hair and a cigarette dangling out of his mouth came over. He looked about as agitated as one could get in the early morning. He flashed his credentials to us; he was FBI. What were they doing here?

"The name's Drew Muldoon, from the local FBI field office. Mr. Thomas, which agent took the shares in?"

He gestured with his thumb at me. "Kyle here took them. Why do you ask?"

"I'm going to need to ask you a few questions," Agent Muldoon said.

My stomach began to twist into knots. "What can I do for you?"

He flipped open his notepad. "Who from Ares Commerce dropped those certificates off with you?"

"Amy Pandemos," I answered.

He sighed and rubbed his head. "Did she say or do anything else while she was here?"

I took a moment before answering - should I tell him everything or not? Muldoon didn't seem like a very useful agent. "She dropped off the certificates and said she just wanted a safe place to keep them. I think she was splitting them up between different brokerage offices."

He quickly penned that down. "Makes sense. Well, I have no cause to take the certificates in, but keep a watch on her. If she comes back, let me know."

He handed me his card.

I placed it in my pocket. "I sure will."

Muldoon walked away, back to the other cops that were on the scene. "What was that all about?" Jeremiah asked.

"I have no idea, but things are getting interesting around here, aren't they?"

"I'm thinking this Ares Commerce is in on it," Jeremiah whispered as Muldoon looked back over.

"In on what?" I asked.

"The conspiracy," he answered.

I just couldn't. Jeremiah was the one who had put that kernel in my mind in the first place. There were no weird flu strains and certainly no Area 51 nonsense. Possibly money laundering and most certainly some sort of financial hokey pokey going on; that my gut told me. However, until I had more proof, if there was any to be found, I was not getting into it. Amy Pandemos was a client and potentially, a very valuable one. I just shook my head as Jeremiah spouted off some more of his crazy thoughts. None that I had any interest in, nope.

Well maybe, just a bit.

"Where there's smoke, there's fire, Kyle. And there's a lot of smoke with GenX. You need to be careful with your dealings with them, okay?" he asked of me.

"I will, sir."

We were finally let into the office and I had four missed calls and two messages; all from Amy. I immediately called her back to reassure her everything was fine. "Don't worry, the certificates are safe; no one was able to penetrate our safe."

"Are you sure?"

"Physical security and clearing are going over the records right now. They checked your stocks first, due to the size and value."

"I'm sorry for questions; losing those certificates would've been a huge blow to my funds," she said further, the fear in her voice beginning to soften.

My heart rate was still pretty high. "If you'd like, why don't you come back down to the office this afternoon and I can show you. We can then go into further details about the block trades you'd like to do," I offered.

Silence for a moment, before, "That's actually a very good idea. I'll clear my calendar. See you in a few hours, Kyle."

That went better than anticipated.

Once the excitement of the morning died down, it was back into my normal groove. Place a buy order for two hundred shares of a terrible pot stock to a college dropout named Piotr, sleep through a few sell orders for an old guy named Walter, the normal stuff, you know? It wasn't until my grinder and fries showed up that I broke out of my stupor of boredom. Was it sad that I missed the excitement from the FBI and break-in this morning?

Maybe my meeting with Amy would provide some action.

I was deleting a bunch of email when Amy graced my presence once again. "Thank you for the invite," she sighed as she sat down in the crappy guest chair I had. "A long afternoon of boring board meetings never seems appealing."

"What board of directors were you meeting with, if I can be so bold?"

"My own, the Ares Commerce board."

Bingo! She was with them. "I've heard of Ares Commerce," I offered nonchalantly.

"I know you have."

"How?"

"Your deep dive searches, your interest in RedKoin and GenX, I know it all. It is my job to know anyone and everyone who looks into me or my company. Don't be so surprised, Kyle," she said as my jaw was probably on the desk by now. "That was the reason I came to this firm, to you. I wanted to see who was so interested in me."

Oh boy.

"I am going to level with you, Kyle. I'm not just the head of Ares Commerce, I'm also the CEO of GenX. Ares is just a way to fund my true passion project, making the world a safer place."

"I didn't expect that," I admitted.

Amy leaned back in her chair, letting her long brown hair dangle backwards. "Kyle, what I'm truly looking for is a partner who understands the financial side of a business, who understands how to make money work for them." She sat back up and rested her arms on my desk. "I need someone I can give total control of Ares Commerce to; someone who won't let me down."

"Whoa, you just met me and-"

"Kyle Carlisle," she cut me off. "Barely graduated high school and had a penchant for misbehaving. Took a job at a local garage for a few years and turned it around. Became interested in investing and signed on as an intern at a small-time fund manager's firm. Passed his SIE, Series 7, and Series 63 licenses in the span of four months. Got a job with Sherwood and quickly rose to the top of the client services and trades department. Now, what were you saying?" she asked with a smile.

It was also like she was reading my life's biography off a Wiki page. "Knowing facts and knowing who I am are two different things," I countered.

"You were a troublemaker because you wanted to destabilize the system, Kyle."

No.

Hell no, that wasn't possible. That was, word for word, the reason I gave my high school principal my senior year for refusing to do an assignment on oppression. "Just who are you, again?"

"I am someone with a lot of power and pull, Kyle. So, let's take a walk, see the operation, and you can tell me how good you are with cryptocurrency," she said.

****

An entire company funded by RedKoin,

I couldn't believe what she had told me while I was there.

To give you a quick synopsis, RedKoin was a type of cryptocurrency that was backed only by blocks of data that computer engineers "mined" from various places. The longer the blockchain, the more secure and valuable the currency was. Almost everyone knew what Bitcoin was, but RedKoin was the newest kid on the blockchain (investor humor there) and was already taking off. It was currently worth, at my last check, at two hundred and eighty-seven dollars per coin. When you thought about how many purchased these coins in huge chunks, whoever created this chain was a very rich individual.

My gut told me that someone close to Amy probably created it.

Back to our conversation: Amy was looking to poach me from Global Options to take over GenX's financial side and help make RedKoin grow. Not only would the company pay for my rent, but the salary that she quoted during our walkthrough of Sherwood was double of what I was currently making.

And I wasn't making peanuts, mind you.

It was her last message that stuck with me. "I know I came here under false pretenses; however, I believe in your abilities. Don't sell yourself short, Kyle."

The reason that line hit me hard was because of how hard I worked to get to where I was. As she was correct in stating, I didn't have the best starts in life and worked day and night to get to where I was.

Did I feel I deserved more?

Absolutely.

Did I want to give up a solid job for something potentially very shady?

That's where it got a bit more muddled.

The cool air of the night was nice for taking a walk and thinking. I promised her that next Monday, I'd come to her office at GenX and sit down for a formal interview. I was kind of surprised at myself for saying yes, as even in the moment, I wasn't very sure about everything. Yet, there I was, compelled to say yes. Maybe that was my subconscious trying to push me to take a chance. At the very least, what harm could come from just an interview?

Yeah, I was worrying for nothing.

4

Market Risk

The risk of losses in positions arising from movements in market prices.

"Muldoon, are you going to go home?"

"Sorry sir, just dealing with a bit of a migraine."

Ever since the raid at War Dog Labs, I'd been dealing with very random, intense migraines. I figured it was my way of dealing with the deaths of Schulte, Taft, and Cleveland. I couldn't believe that Taft and Cleveland had been in league with Venus Typhon in a money laundering scheme and corporate espionage. Apparently, millions of dollars had been funneled into Cayman accounts, as well as a bunch of tech and pending patents being stolen from a small cap tech company, GenX.

"Something doesn't add up," I mumbled to myself.

"What's that, Agent Muldoon?"

My new partner, Agent Chrystle Marron, sat a cup of coffee down on my desk. "Thanks."

"You going to tell me what you're working on?"

I hadn't taken her over to Global Options today, deciding to look into that myself. That probably wasn't the best of moves; I could use a second set of eyes. "I'm trying to connect the dots. Something in the back of my mind, I can't place what, is telling me that what happened at War Dog is connected to the botched robbery this morning."

Marron picked up my case report from this morning. "It looks pretty cut and dry, huh?"

"Exactly! No evidence of who tried to do this and they left a bunch of valuable information there. They were only concerned with the stock certificates that were kept in their vault."

She flipped to the next page. "GenX - the one company that gained the most from your bust of War Dog," she observed.

"Everything about GenX looks on the up and up. I mean, they are experimenting with vaccines for weird bat viruses that could come out of China, but other than that, there's not much there," I sighed.

"Maybe we need to go take a look at War Dog Labs again. You and Schulte were under fire and were double-crossed. No one would be expecting us to head on back over, now that it's been over a month since the raid."

That wasn't a bad idea. I snapped up my case files and the coffee. The two of us headed out the field office door and towards the Charger that was assigned for my use. Considering it was pretty late, the ride over from the field office to War Dog only took about ten minutes. Once we got out of the car, the migraine hit me again.

"You okay, Muldoon?"

"Yeah, just need a minute."

"Did you get a concussion or something?" she asked.

The doctors had given me a pretty clean bill of health; just a few bruised ribs and damaged pride. "I think it's just the stress and everything that goes with losing a partner."

"Damn, I'm sorry, Muldoon."

“It’s okay. I’ll grieve for Schulte once I unwind this whole mystery.”

“Once we unwind this. I’m with you until the end, Drew.”

That actually made me feel a bit better. As we entered the building, “I think we need to go to the third floor.”

The power was out in the building, so we turned on the flashlights and hit the stairwell. When we passed the door to the second floor, I felt a pang of survivor’s guilt. A big chunk of me felt as if I should have been the one to die that night, not Schulte. She was a young, good agent. I’d already come to terms that this job was probably going to get me killed. The fact that it was someone I’d grown to respect and viewed as a bright light in this damn job, that’s what hurt the most.

As we entered the third floor, I finally got a good look at the area. My first visit was just to deal with two shooters; this time it was to get answers. The third floor was boxy, with cement floors and UV lights hung from the ceiling. Besides the broken windows from my quick kills of the gunmen, the only real distinct features were the three large security doors that lined the perimeter. There were two on the west side of the building and one on the east side. Something was gnawing at me to go towards the door on the east side. As I approached, it had a complicated looking lock pad installed right beside it. With the power being out, I hoped this unorthodox idea I had worked.

I pistol whipped the box, knocking it from the wall.

"Got some anger issues there, Muldoon?"

I grabbed the large handle on the door, hoping it gave way as I ignored Marron's comments. Just my luck, the handle went down and the door swung forward, just a little bit. It was a heavy, steel door that took some muscle to get all the way open. It was too damn dark inside to see anything, so we began flashing our lights all around. I wasn't the biggest science fiction movie fan in the world, but this had all the hallmarks of a mad scientist's lab.

"I can't imagine this is the kind of lab where pharmaceuticals are made," I observed.

"I'm right there with you."

The light from my flashlight got in range of the back wall, illuminating it. Good God - there were chains bolted into the cement and what looked like blood all around. "Jesus, Marron, what do you think happened here?"

She took a moment before answering, allowing the eerie silence to send chills down my spine. "I think we stumbled across some sort of torture chamber."

"Do you believe in aliens?"

"If you would've asked me about five minutes ago, I'd say you need to seek help. But after seeing this, I was thinking more along the lines of demons, but either would work," Marron answered.

There was another door, in the corner. This one was smaller, made of wood. I hesitated for a split second, not that keen to see what prizes awaited us behind door number two. As soon as I pulled this door open, we both gasped. A man, a very thin man with a gaunt, bearded face, a few unique tattoos across his chest, and a long litany of scars running over the parts of him not covered up by the dirty white shorts and shirt was just sitting there. If there was ever a picture-perfect example of what starvation looked like, it was him.

And he was alive.

"Are you okay?" I asked as I rushed down to his position.

Something along the lines of laughter came out of his chapped, cracked lips. "I'm about… to die and the… humans find me."

Listening to his hoarse voice was like nails on a chalkboard.

"What do you mean 'humans' were the one to find you? Are you not human?" Marron asked.

When he coughed this time, blood began to streak down his dirty face. "We… are cosmic beings," he choked out. "Old... ones before your... time."

"Call an ambulance."

"I don't think that'll be necessary, Muldoon."

The man's skin began to turn ashen. As life left his body, it crumbled into dust that drifted away, returning to the Earth from where it came.

"Ash to ash, they like to say."

I couldn't take my eyes off the spot where everything just happened. Bodies just don't die and decompose into thin air. "Cosmic beings, old ones; what did we just stumble upon?"

Marron helped me back to my feet. Her eyes told the same story mine did. "I have no idea, but no one will believe us. Maybe we keep this one under wraps until we get more proof."

That was a damn good idea.

I wasn't hopeful, but maybe the third floor had more secrets to unveil.

The doors on the west side led into what you would've expected to see in a pharmaceutical drug making building. These labs were filled with test tubes and other gadgets chemists would've used to mix and match crap. The only thing extraordinary about either lab, because all the real good stuff had been taken or destroyed by now, were the names etched into the walls. The first lab was named Project: Aphrodite Paradox, and the second lab was called Project: Hades Pathogen. Again, as you probably figured out by now, I was no scientist and didn't pretend to know what the hell was going on, but even the term pathogen meant something to me.

"Hades was the ruler of the underworld," Marron whispered.

"They were creating a virus to kill."

I walked along the desks. The Aphrodite Paradox; that sounded so familiar, but I couldn't place it. In fact, as I thought about it, the migraine began to creep back in. I didn't need that distraction at this moment, not when I needed to be focused. As I was about to finish my sweep of this row, a yellow file folder caught my eye, lying under the second to last desk. The only reason I saw it was because of the migraine, forcing me to look downwards. I'd developed that reaction to them when I began to rub my temples, hoping for some relief. It was about damn time they came in handy.

"Marron, come check this out," I yelled as I stood back up.

Together, we looked over the information. The papers I skimmed over talked about the breakthroughs in the Project: Hades Pathogen and how they could be taken to the next step, clinical trials. If that wasn't scary enough, wanting to run trials on some sort of death virus, the company name on the header wasn't War Dog Labs - it was

GenX Biolabs. Of course! War Dog Labs hadn't stolen proprietary information. They'd been created by GenX as a fall company.

"I'm not sure what you found, Muldoon, but you should read this."

Marron handed me her papers while I passed mine back to her. It was clear it was talking about the Aphrodite Paradox. Human trials had already taken place and the project was ready to enter its last phase, incorporation. That wasn't the scariest part, however.

As this host's body has begun fighting back for control, we are ready to move into the final phase. The bait has been set and the perfect host will soon be here. Once I have taken control of her body, I can focus all my efforts into distribution of the red coins as we prepare to bring the Hades Pathogen into fruition.

"It's clear to me we've either stumbled into something alien or occult," I said with heavy, labored breathing. "We can't take this back to the field office. They'll think I've snapped and taken you along for the ride."

"After what I've seen tonight, that is too damn risky for sure."

We put all the papers back in the file folder, swept the remainder of the third floor before leaving the building. We didn't say much until we stopped at the 24/7 Diner. This late, the only thing that they had on the television was the news and it was in the middle of the financial portion of the program, talking about market risk. Neither of us were quite ready to share our thoughts, still processing the information and the encounter with the *cosmic being*. It wasn't until the coffee and the key lime pie were sat in front of us that we finally spoke about what we discovered.

"How do we get a warrant to search GenX if we can't show anyone this information?" Marron questioned, visibly frustrated with the situation. "Our only witness disappeared into a puff of smoke."

It'd actually been dust, but I wasn't going to correct her. It was the exact same problem I'd been trying to wrap my head around since we left War Dog. "I don't think we need one, to be honest." A smile started to crawl onto my face. "Nothing like being good agents and just doing a follow up with them the day after someone tried to steal their stock certificates."

"That's why they pay you the big bucks," Marron chuckled, amused with her own little joke of bureau pay scales.

"I won't ask for a raise yet. Let's hope they are willing to see us."

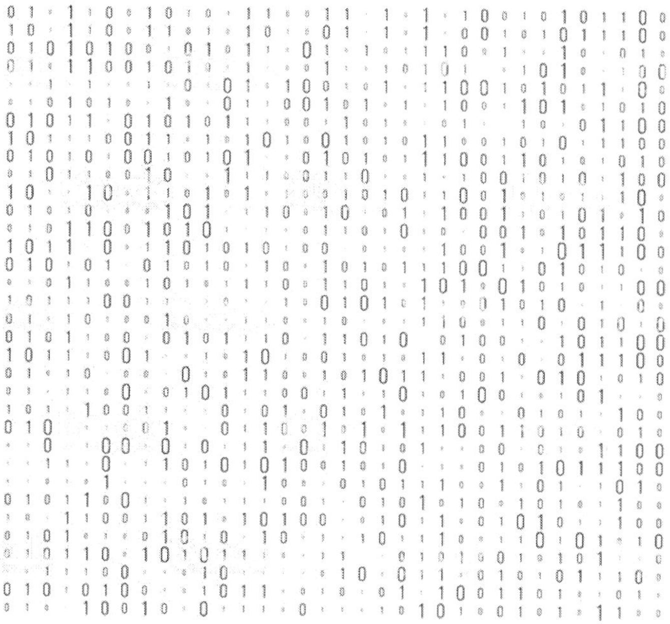

5

Cryptocurrency

A digital currency in which encryption techniques are used to regulate the generation of units of currency.

The weekend flew by.

As I sat in the waiting room in the GenX lobby, my nerves were starting to get the better of my composure. I promised myself on Friday night that

I wouldn't psyche myself out by doing more research into Ares, GenX, or Amy. Instead, I focused all of my energy on video games and cheap beer. It mostly worked; there was almost an incident on Saturday night, close to midnight. I woke up; I was having a dream, I think. I couldn't remember much of what happened in the dream, but I had an overwhelming feeling to search the internet for the Greek gods? Why in the hell would I ever need to do that?

I went back to sleep and chalked it up to the beer and video games.

Other than that odd moment, nothing drastic happened and I didn't chicken out of my interview.

"Kyle Carlisle, Miss Pandemos is ready to see you."

As soon as the receptionist called my name, my game face came on. I had plenty of questions and I am sure she did, too. As I walked up the stairs in the open lobby, I saw Amy sitting behind her desk in the glass office. She motioned for me to come in and the door closed behind me on its own. That was a pretty boss door, with quiet, yet powerful gas struts that seamlessly closed the door the moment someone let go. One day, I'd have an office with a door like that.

It exuded power.

"Good morning, Kyle, I hope you had a pleasant weekend."

"Can't complain - living the college dream at my old age," I laughed.

"You can't be what, twenty-eight, maybe twenty-nine?" she asked.

"I turn thirty this August."

"Just a year younger than myself, I like that. Us millennials are the ones to take knowledge forward and need to work together to ensure that. But," she added, "we must never forget the knowledge from those who preceded us."

"That sounds like something my dad would've said."

"Are you close with him?"

"Both of my parents died some years back."

"I'm so sorry," she quickly said, her face going red.

"I came to grips with it a long time ago. No need to apologize."

After the semi-awkward beginning to the interview, the rest of it went smoothly. She asked me about my experience with Sherwood, my own financial experience managing my own funds, and some questions regarding cryptocurrency. There was nothing out of the ordinary. She was a focused and driven businesswoman from everything I could tell from the conversation, looking for someone trustworthy to look over a very high value, highly volatile aspect of her business.

"I know you've heard of RedKoin, Kyle, but, what do you know about it?"

"What I know, or what I think I know?" She just smiled, not directing me one way or another. "What I know is that it's one of the hottest coins out there on the market right now."

"And what do you think you know?" she prodded.

"What I think is, this coin was founded by GenX as a way to save the IPO that failed. I think that you didn't expect GenX to turn around so fast and you got lucky with two gold mines, instead of just one," I finished up nicely.

She actually began clapping. "That is the intuition and speculation that I was hoping I'd see. You are right," she agreed. "RedKoin was developed by a group of my engineers here and funded through Ares. With these revenue funds coming in faster than even I anticipated, GenX will be able to do all the good work this world needs."

Amy had mentioned this *work* before. I knew GenX was a biotech lab, but I didn't understand much of what they did. "I understand Ares Commerce very well, as a financial guy. What I don't understand is what GenX does?"

With that question, her eyes really lit up, more than I'd seen ever talking about anything financial related. "We are working on a few projects here, projects that will change the world if we are successful."

"Friend to friend, care to elaborate?" I was trying to get the inside scoop.

It worked! "We have three ongoing projects; the Hades Pathogen, the Aphrodite Paradox, and our newest project, the Khronos Sickle. Each one designed to breakthrough ceilings in medicine that we never thought were possible."

"I'm just surprised someone with your background in finance is so taken with modern medicine and such."

"Let's just say when Ares bought this place last month, a new sense of duty overcame me."

That was an answer I could appreciate. For some reason, the names of the projects she rattled off stirred some kind of deja vu. I didn't necessarily know where or what they meant, but my brain couldn't help but repeating them. Hades, Aphrodite, Kronos? What did they mean and why did they feel familiar?

"Let's cut to the chase, now that we spent some time dancing around the subject."

"What chase is that?" I asked.

"Money, of course! What I'm prepared to offer you to run the RedKoin part of my ever-growing empire should be quite competitive in today's job market." She opened her desk drawer, plucked out a file folder, and slid it across the desk to me.

When I opened it up, I nearly choked. “Is this right?”

“I hope the package isn’t too low or not comprehensive enough.”

There was nothing low or not comprehensive enough about it. The base salary was one hundred and ten thousand dollars a year. The benefits included full coverage of health care, dental, a matching 401k, and a stipend for rent. No, this package was far more than anyone in my position could’ve ever asked for.

“When you told me last week that I’d be making double, this is way more than I anticipated seeing,” I told her honestly.

“With the two of us working together, Kyle, we can ensure that everyone in the world has access not only to the wealth of RedKoin, but soon, the fruition of what we’re working on here.”

Without even a second to consider, “I accept.”

****

“I can’t say I’m surprised, Kyle. I always worried someone would snatch you away,” Jeremiah responded to my two weeks’ notice offering. “It looks like you’re going to get a little vacation before you start over there with GenX.”

In the broker world, no one ever let you actually work your two weeks when you gave your notice. The fear was that you'd take clients with you, wherever you went. Even though I was going to be officially working for GenX and not Ares Commerce, since I was working in their issuing department (the place where RedKoins and potential follow-up offerings for their stock were issued), technically, I wasn't leaving the brokerage industry. Jeremiah was about to walk me out after I collected all my stuff.

It was a good thing I didn't have much.

It only took about ten minutes to clear my desk, say bye to my friends, and drive off from Global Options. It felt surreal, leaving the place that I really established myself at. I liked everyone I worked with, I enjoyed my clients, even the annoying ones. Now, I had two weeks to really think about what I'd be doing for Amy and GenX. I'd be in charge of hawking RedKoins to investors and making sure that everything done with the cryptocurrency was to make it accessible to everyone. Amy was adamant about getting RedKoin into the virtual wallets of every person we could.

When I pulled into my parking spot at the apartment complex, I saw something on my door. I quickly parked and walked over just to see; I'd paid my rent, right? As I pulled the letter off of my door, I saw it was a handwritten letter and it was very cryptic.

"Meet me at the corner of 10th and Long. Come alone - now."

I immediately pulled out my cell phone and called the police's non-emergency number to report that a note had been put on my door. The operator, while sympathetic, told me it was not a crime to leave a note taped to the door and that I just needed to be vigilant. I was pretty frustrated when I hung up; the hope to have a cop come over and canvas the area now seemed pretty unrealistic when I thought about it.

When I entered my apartment, it was clear that my visitor had stopped at the front door. Nothing was moved or disturbed. Not that I had much, mind you. My possessions were basically a beaten-up couch that I refused to part with, my big screen television (complete with sound-bar and gaming systems), and some odds and ends here and there. I didn't even have a dining table. I liked a simple, streamlined approach to living and I liked my rather comfortable apartment set-up. I had no doubts that this wouldn't even take up half of the housing stipend I was about to get, which made me smile a little. My dad had taught me much, but his biggest life lesson was to never go overboard with junk. *If you don't use it at least once every week, what's the point?* was his life's mantra to clutter and unnecessary spending.

I quickly changed from my dress clothes and into more appropriate jeans and a hoodie combination for doing something stupid. Yep, I was going to see just who came to visit me at my apartment and left behind such a cryptic note. Before I could even talk myself out of something so dumb, I was back out the door and into my car. I kept my mind focused on the task at hand, trying not to let any weird thoughts creep in.

You know the ones; what if I'd just accepted a job with aliens?

Nope, not going to go down that rabbit hole again.

I parked my car and briskly walked over to the corner. People were out and about, walking around town to get to lunch, shopping, or wherever. I had absolutely no idea who I was looking for; I just hoped they knew what I looked like and came to me.

"Kyle, follow me," a man's voice behind me said softly, but was pretty friendly.

I turned around and saw FBI agent Drew Muldoon walking towards O'Shea's Bar and Grille. I kept up as he didn't say another word until the two of us were inside and seated at a booth in the back. He took off his fedora and ran his hand through his black hair that had random grays sprinkled in. He looked tired, like a man who hadn't slept in a very long time.

"Are you okay, Agent Muldoon?"

"Yeah, I'm just glad you came, Kyle."

A waiter came over and took our orders. Muldoon said he was buying and got us two beers and an order of nachos. "The reason I reached out in such an old school way is I need an inside person. I know you were offered a job with GenX and you accepted it."

"How did you know that?" I asked politely. So far, he'd been nothing but pleasant.

"I'm an FBI agent, Kyle," he pointed out correctly. "It is my business to know everything about my investigation."

What was he investigating? "Are you looking into GenX?"

"What do you know about War Dog Labs?" he answered my question with one of his own.

"The lab that was apparently stealing from GenX? Not much," I answered truthfully. "Just what I read in the papers and heard through the grapevine in regards to GenX's rebound in the market. I figured it was just a bunch of half-truths and lies, to be honest."

He paused for a second as our drinks and food showed up. He grabbed his beer and threw back about half before he went on. "Kid, the papers don't even know a quarter of it. Before I get into that, I need to know I can trust you with as much of the truth as I can divulge."

"Agent Muldoon, with all due respect, I just took a job at GenX. You're putting me in a very awkward situation."

In between bites of nacho, "I know. Trust me, I know. But, once you get the full picture, there ain't no going back," he warned.

"What do you need me to do to earn your trust?"

He pulled out a USB drive. "I need this drive to find its way onto Amy Pandemos' computer and get everything listed about the Aphrodite Paradox."

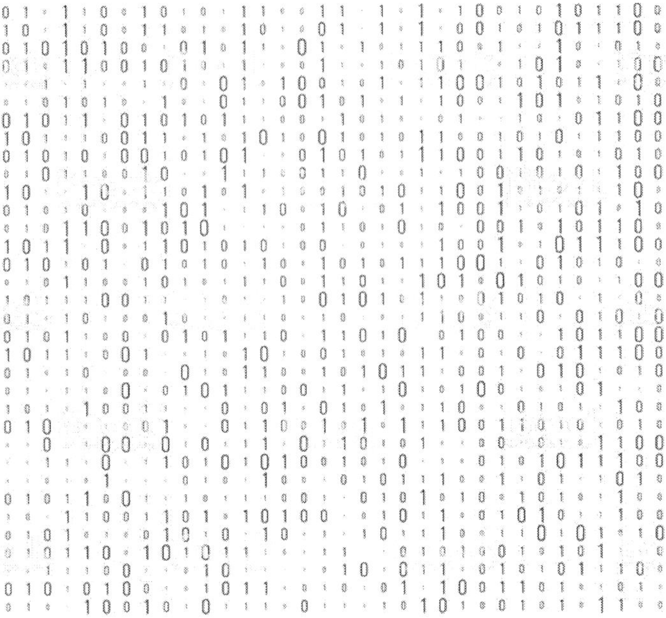

6

Tender Offer

A type of public takeover bid constituting an offer to purchase some or all of shareholders' shares in a corporation.

There was no time like the present to do what I was about to do. Muldoon’s offer of giving me real knowledge about the situation was just too tempting to ignore. Damnit! I did the one thing I told myself I wasn't going to. Why did I keep getting wrapped up in the mystery that surrounded GenX? It was almost like something was pulling me towards this nonsense.

Ughhh...

But if Muldoon had tangible information that could be helpful to me, I needed to take the chance and get it. Even if it got me in trouble with my new employer, the risk was worth it. As I walked into GenX's lobby, I felt more at ease now than I did earlier today for the job interview. I smiled and waved at the receptionist the moment she saw me.

"Hello, I was curious if Ms. Pandemos was in the office?"

"Kyle Carlisle, right?" she asked me.

"Yes ma'am."

She picked up her desk phone and dialed out. "Yes ma'am, Kyle Carlisle is here to see you." There was silence and head nodding as Amy was answering her. When she finished, "Thank you Ms. Pandemos, I will send him up and let him know."

The receptionist explained to me that Amy was in a meeting and she'd be finished in about fifteen minutes. She led me to her office where I took a seat and crossed my legs. The USB that Muldoon asked me to place in her computer was still jangling in my pocket.

"My tech contact assured me that if you just plug this in, the USB will do the rest. As soon as it stops blinking, it'll be finished. I'm counting on you, kid," he had told me.

As soon as the receptionist was out of sight, no one was around to see me plug it in. I wasn't the most graceful person in the world, but I got the job done. I was back in my seat in no time, just in case anyone walked by and saw me. The moment the USB was fully plugged in, just like Muldoon had told me, it began to blink red. I had set a timer on my watch for ten minutes, just in case Amy finished her meeting early and came in. That would be an awkward conversation before she called the cops, I was betting.

Now the nerves began to act up.

My foot began tapping on the floor as the USB just kept blinking. Time seemed to slow down to almost a complete halt. Each time I checked the timer, it seemed like a second or two would tick away. C'mon, I thought to myself. How slow can FBI tech really work?

Well it was a government agency, I reminded myself.

Over the next few minutes, I did my best to calm myself. I thought about baseball, music, and even about my current living situation. With the new job, barring I didn't get fired for this stunt, should I upgrade my apartment? Maybe a sound system, or even an upgrade to the fridge and microwave. What broke me out of my thought train was the sound of heels clicking along the marble floor. Oh damn! I looked over at the USB and saw that the dumb thing had stopped blinking. With reflexes faster than I'd ever experienced before, I yanked it out and got back into my seat moments before Amy walked in.

"Kyle! Good to see you, though a few days too soon, I think."

This was the part I hadn't given much thought to, for very clear reasons. Getting the USB drive and the information was the hardest part of the task, so I thought. "I had a weird meeting at lunch," I spouted out.

"How so?" she asked curiously.

"An FBI agent, Muldoon I think, began asking me questions about RedKoin in regards to potential insider trading for GenX shares. I told him that was nonsense, but I guess he'd been looking into it from some of the trades I'd placed at Global Options."

"Muldoon," she whispered. That was curious. "If he ever bothers you again, have him call me directly and I will put him in contact with our legal team. We vetted you thoroughly before I even approached you. How dare some snarky agent make assumptions like that," she finished.

It was clear that she knew him, but Muldoon made no mention of ever meeting her. "I sure will.

I just wanted to make sure you knew what was going on so there were no surprises," I responded.

"I was right with my decision, Kyle. Thank you for your honesty and trust in me to tell me right away."

"Absolutely. Hopefully, I can enjoy the rest of my forced vacation before I start with GenX."

"Global Options let you go early?"

"Yeah, due to the fear I'd take clients with me, or something like that."

She began chuckling which built into a full-on laugh. "They really thought the number of clients you could bring over would be significant? Oh my," she sighed.

I was under the impression, in my mind at least, that this is where the meeting would have ended. Instead, Amy got up and retrieved a bottle of scotch from a cabinet behind her desk. She poured two shot glasses full and brought one over to me. She sat in another one of the guest chairs and offered her glass for a toast.

"You know why it's a good day to drink, Kyle?"

"Any day is a good day to drink," I said, after taking a sip of the very smooth, very expensive drink in my hand. "But, I'm guessing there's a reason for this?"

"I'm putting together a tender offer for Covid Technological. We met with the regulators today and the paperwork's been approved."

It was my turn to start chuckling. "I guess I'll be getting an email about that. I own two hundred shares of Covid. I bought them a couple years back when they were barely over a dollar."

"Believe it or not, they have tech that my scientists tell me will change the game, once combined with our research. Like I said," she went on with another clink of the glasses, "we are going to change the world."

After another glass of scotch, that's when the meeting finally ended. I waited until I was far away from the building before I called Muldoon on the number he provided. I went over the whole encounter with him, from the successful porting of the USB to the odd feeling that Amy knew him personally. He proclaimed to have never met her, going as far as to say he'd never even heard of her until recent developments in his case crossed paths with her.

"We need to meet, Kyle, but it needs to be done right. Tonight, at around eight, my partner will be picking you up. It'll look like a date to anyone who might be observing you, so dress appropriately. Once you're with Agent Marron, we'll figure it out from there."

"Anything I need to do until then?"

"Just keep a low profile and hold onto that USB."

I went right home and locked the door as soon as I entered. As the afternoon stretched into evening, I was on pins and needles waiting for Muldoon's partner to get there. I'd be safe with the FBI. Chances were that Amy had no idea what I'd done and I was being paranoid for no reason, yet, a part of my brain told me to take precautions. It was hard to ignore that survival instinct, even if I thought it might be overkill.

Around seven, I got dressed, nicely as Muldoon suggested. I picked a pair of jeans that I'd spent way too much on right after I'd gotten my job at Global Options, a black button-down that had the sleeves rolled up three times, and my leather shoes. If anyone knew me at all, they'd know that I'd only take out my leather shoes for a special occasion. These weren't meant to see the elements very often.

As I was giving my hair one last combing, the doorbell rang. I patted my pocket, making sure the USB drive was still there and gathered my courage. When I opened my door, I didn't know what I'd been expecting, but it wasn't this. Agent Marron (I think that's what Muldoon had said her name was) was a straight up bombshell. Her reddish-brown hair was curly, she was dressed to impress, and I was ninety-nine percent sure that her jeans put mine to shame. In her black heels, she was just a tad taller than me too.

I was at a loss for words.

"Kyle, right?" she broke the ice. "I'm Chrystle. It's a pleasure to meet you, finally."

"It's great to meet you, too."

I couldn't help but notice the '67 charcoal black Mustang parked along the curb. The bright white pony decals really made it stand out. "You like what you see?" I wasn't sure if she was referring to herself or the car. That's when Agent Marron jabbed me in the shoulder. "I'm just teasing you, Kyle. Lighten up," she advised.

"I'll do my best," I said.

"Well, we've got a reservation in fifteen, so let's get a move on it."

Not long after I got in the Mustang, we were driving down the highway. At this point, it felt safe to talk. "Muldoon's told me a lot without telling me anything at all. Can I at least get a little bit of an understanding of the situation?"

"I'd like to tell you everything, but I'm not sure words do the situation justice. We're dealing with something..." she paused, as if looking for the right word. "Extraordinary," she finished.

We made small talk after that. I realized trying to push the issue would probably just piss off an FBI agent and I certainly didn't want to do that. Turns out Agent Marron and I had a lot in common. We both enjoyed classic rock, ice hockey, and she was a bit of a casual investor. The last ten or so minutes of the drive were spent discussing the merits of cryptocurrency. She was a bit of a skeptic, and rightfully so.

"What I don't understand is, nothing backs it. Basically, it is Monopoly money that somehow the world has gone crazy for."

While I agreed with her theory, "Trust me, at this point, even the newest of crypto's like RedKoin is probably more stable than the U.S. dollar. When you think about it, the dollar isn't even backed by gold anymore."

Her fingers tapped on the steering wheel. "Funny you should mention RedKoin. That's one of the points of the investigation I can tell you about."

"Considering I'm the new RedKoin issuer supervisor for GenX, I'd love to actually know something tangible."

She reached over to the glove box and opened it. Inside, there was a manilla file folder with RedKoin written in black marker at the top. I took it out and opened it. The fact that the FBI had an entire folder already filled with RedKoin information didn't make me feel all that great with my job security.

I sure hoped Global Options would take me back after this.

However, the information in the file folder didn't contain financial information, or even potential information on the blockchain that had created RedKoin. No, it contained information about novel diseases, corporate espionage, and murder. From what I could tell, RedKoin was backing projects at GenX labs to both produce and cure different strands of viruses, gaining the profit off the vaccines and government grants. Someone had circled the word *coincidence* by the report on War Dog Labs.

I needed to know the full story.

Agent Marron turned off the main road, onto a dirt path that wound around. "One of our safe houses is up here," she explained.

When we turned the last corner, the safe house came into view. But something was wrong. The door was off the hinges and it looked like the exterior may have been covered in bullet holes. Marron skidded to a stop out front, grabbing her gun as she exited the car. She motioned for me to stay put as she began to walk inside, slowly. I should've listened, as she was a trained FBI agent, however, it seemed like a bad idea to let her go in, alone.

I wish I had stayed in the car.

Lying in a pool of blood was Agent Drew Muldoon.

He was very much dead.

7

Margin Call

A demand by a broker that an investor deposit more cash or securities to cover possible losses.

Kyle Carlisle was in good hands, now that Agent Marron had just left. I was still reeling from the shock that she wasn't actually FBI, but from another agency sent in to assist me with this case. I didn't think anyone else but me had the kind of in-depth knowledge that I possessed. She had seemed genuinely shocked by what we'd found at War Dog Labs; at least I knew I could trust her. She promised me once Kyle was here, she'd explain everything further.

I'd used that same line on the kid earlier in the day.

The FBI safe house we were setting up as our home base was located on the outskirts of the city. It was actually a safe house from the seventies that was no longer in use, and therefore, no longer on record. I'd found out about this place earlier in my career. Besides Agent Marron now, the only other person who knew I used it from time to time was my former partner, and friend, Agent Schulte.

Her death still bothered me.

Losing a partner was never easy, but the way it happened... Something just didn't add up in my mind. The events of the night, they didn't feel real. Obviously, they had to be real, as I was there and my memory served me right in recalling everything. I just couldn't shake this feeling. Hell, I couldn't even really describe what or why I had this feeling.

My phone rang. I wasn't expecting to hear back from Marron so soon, but when I held it up, the number that came across was blocked. "Hello," I grumbled.

"Agent Muldoon," a woman's voice answered. "How dare you interfere with Kyle Carlisle's well-being."

"Who the hell is this?" I asked, very annoyed about being questioned by this unknown lady.

"Amy Pandemos, or maybe you know me better as Venus Typhon."

Just like that, whatever drug or trick that had been used to cloud my memory vanished. I was seeing the world clearly for this first time since that awful night. I remembered exactly what happened to Taft, Cleveland, and to my partner. "You bitch, I don't know how you took control of Schulte, but damnit, I am going to find you and I am going to kill you."

"Many have tried over my very long life, Agent Muldoon. I honestly believed you might be able to pull it off, too. So, it's very much a shame I have to kill you tonight."

"We'll see about that," I growled.

"Unfortunately, you made the calculated error of bringing Kyle into this. He's so much more important than you realize, and I just can't have you messing this up."

That's when the phone cut off.

And that's when two black SUVs pulled up to the safe house. I had my Glock on me, plus two hunting rifles that were stored here with plenty of ammo. Whoever was in those SUVs was about to get a very warm welcome. I grabbed the Mossberg Maverick and hid behind the small kitchen island. I had a clear shot of the front door and the window. There were no windows behind me, and no other entry points. The design of this place was perfect - bottleneck the intruders and take them out one by one.

The door was knocked off of its hinges by a blast from the outside. The shotgun had a five-round cartridge in it. These boys were in for a very big surprise. The first man entered, wearing all black. I stood up and pumped the shotgun right before I pulled the trigger. The impact hit his chest and sent him backwards, out of the safe house. There was no doubt about it, he was dead. The second and third men followed quickly, trying to get shots off before I could give them the same fate that their accomplice just received.

I was able to put down one of the two attackers, but the third got a shot off and hit me in the shoulder. I'd been shot before and it was a pain I knew all too well. I bit down on my lips and took down the third gunman. I was expecting another attacker, but none came. It was only when I heard a bullhorn click, "Agent, there's no way out of this except in a body bag. Come out and we'll make it quick."

"Screw you," I yelled back, unsure if they could actually hear me.

"You got two minutes, Agent. After that, it'll be much worse for you."

I reloaded the shotgun and made sure the Glock was ready. What these idiots didn't know was that their last minutes were upon them. The moment they walked in the door; they'd be the ones pushing up daisies. I glanced at my watch really quick, just to see how long Marron had been gone. Good God - only five minutes had passed. I was in this all by myself. I could've called for backup, but I didn't want anyone to know about the safe house and even if I felt the need, the closest agents were probably thirty to forty minutes away.

No one was going to push me around.

I'd set a two-minute timer on my watch. The moment it went off, I pumped the shotgun and blew away the fool who tried to bum rush into the safe house. The next guy behind him, this guy came with a plan. I imagined this was the last attacker and probably the guy leading this hit. He rolled into the house and immediately took cover behind the couch that was off to the right. He used the irregular shape of it to try and take potshots at me with his gun, knowing I couldn't get a clear shot at him from the angle I was at.

I put down the Mossberg and grabbed my Glock. "You're in my house, sunshine. This isn't going to go well for you."

"You got it all wrong, Agent. You're the one who has no options left."

A strategic gun fight broke out between the two of us. Neither of us could get a good angle on the other, however, both of us were able to keep the other from changing positions. We were both safe and pinned down, all in one. The only way this was going to end was for someone to do something either brave or stupid.

I grabbed the shotgun and ran. My assailant saw an opportunity and waited for me to get just out in the open before he fired two rounds. The first missed, but the second caught me in the thigh. The wound burned as my quad eased up, wanting me to stop from continuing. I wouldn't let it. I got to the other side of the room and turned on him. One pump and one pull of the trigger; this nightmare was over.

That's when I slumped over on the floor, the two bullet holes in my body beginning to throb more and more with each passing second. With my adrenaline gone, that was to be expected. I pushed myself to a sitting position on the floor, against the wall, and took a few deep breaths. The moment Agent Marron returned with Kyle, we'd be able to put a plan together,

"Bravo, Agent Muldoon. I wasn't sure if you'd go easily into the night or if I'd have to be the one to dispose of you."

When I looked up, even with a new hairstyle, different haircut, and designer clothes, I recognized my partner anywhere. "What did you do to Rebecca?" I asked.

"I'm just borrowing her body for the time being," Venus Typhon answered. It was most disturbing to hear her voice come from my partner's body.

"Just what are you, Venus? An alien? A demon?"

She wagged a finger at me. "Venus is dead, Agent Muldoon, remember?" She chuckled at her own, sick joke. "I'm Amy Pandemos now."

"You didn't answer my question."

"Agent Muldoon, do you ever look up at night and get lost in the stars? Don't you ever wonder what omnipotent beings might be out there, waiting in the shadows?"

This wasn't getting anywhere. "So, you're an alien." It wasn't a question this time.

"Heavens no - I've lived on this planet longer than the human race has."

Now we were getting somewhere. "Ha, you sound like some delusional god," I egged on.

"I am not delusional, Agent Muldoon, but I am a god."

In an instant, Rebecca disappeared and standing in front of me was the vision of a god. Words would do no justice describing the woman in front of me, but, as quickly as she appeared, she disappeared.

Back as Rebecca, "My real name is Aphrodite, Agent Drew Muldoon. You might know me as the Greek goddess of love, beauty, pleasure, and procreation. What you might not know is I'm also the goddess of spite and jealousy."

What she was saying was total nonsense, or at least, should have been total nonsense. I pointed my Glock at her and fired. As I expected, the bullet never even touched her. "I guess you aren't lying."

Aphrodite acted as if my test shot never even happened. "Millennia ago, Zeus ordered my execution for my infidelity to my husband, Hephaestus. Never mind that Zeus had more affairs and children than anyone, he wanted to make a statement about a woman's place in his world. No one, not my husband or the god I had an affair with, Ares, stood up for me. The only one to object was Hades, ordering his brother to stand down. Zeus banished him to Tartarus and used his lightning bolt to strike me dead, or so he thought."

For a fleeting moment, I felt a pang of sympathy for this body snatching psychopath. "How does ancient history translate into your crimes today?"

"In their arrogance, most of the gods got themselves killed. Zeus' bolt may have killed my true form, but my spirit lingered all these years, planning. What I needed was Hades' spirit to finally be released from Tartarus, so that I could find him and together, we would start a new order," she told me with great zeal. "Unfortunately, his spirit came back as a human, one Kyle Carlisle and he has no memories of who he truly is."

"And the man you were holding hostage at War Dog Labs?"

"Oh him? Ares finally got his just desserts for betraying me and then hiding like the true coward he was," she said, rage trembled just under the surface.

The pieces were beginning to fall in place. "What I don't get is the cryptocurrency and the bio-tech firms. Just what are you hoping to accomplish?"

She kicked the shotgun away from me and sat down, right beside me. "Between being a thorn in my side for months now and your sheer determination not to die, you've been one of my most challenging adversaries, Agent Muldoon. Before your death, I will enlighten you to my true plan."

I wasn't surprised I was going to die.

In fact, death would hopefully bring a peace I hadn't felt in a long time.

"Over the years, the one thing I learned to trust is the power of the herd mentality. What humans have failed to grasp for so many centuries are that their beliefs fuel so much of what happens. Now it's my turn to shift that belief to me. First, I'll give them wealth, in the form of my traitorous lover's image. Then when my self-developed plague hits, I will give them the cure."

As much as I wanted to rebuke her plans, we were greedy, selfish creatures. "And how does Carlisle play into this?"

"Unlike me, who still needs to regain her true form, Kyle is very much Hades reborn. Once his eyes are opened to the truth, his touch will be the final ingredient I need for both the plague and the vaccine," she finished.

Judging by the time on the wall clock, my life was just about expired. "One last question - how does Schulte get her body back?"

She rubbed my face, lovingly. "She cares for you deeply, Muldoon. I will be honest, there's a chance I will never regain my goddess form back. If that's the case, then I am afraid I will stay here until the time comes to switch again. I know you wanted a better answer, but you deserve the truth."

Aphrodite stood up and pulled me up with her. By now, I was very much feeling the effects of the gunshots, plus her godly energy. There was no reason to fight back. She laid me down in the middle of the room and snapped her fingers. Shadows emerged from the ground and took the four corpses away, just like they'd never been here. From my vantage point, I could still see out the window and the SUVs disappeared, too.

She truly was a god.

"Those fools will not have the same fate you will. You're a brave, noble man, Drew Muldoon. May your days be full of bliss in the Elysian Fields."

Death did not hurt, nor was I scared. As Aphrodite shot me in the chest, a warmth came over me and a feeling I hadn't had in a very long time...

Serenity.

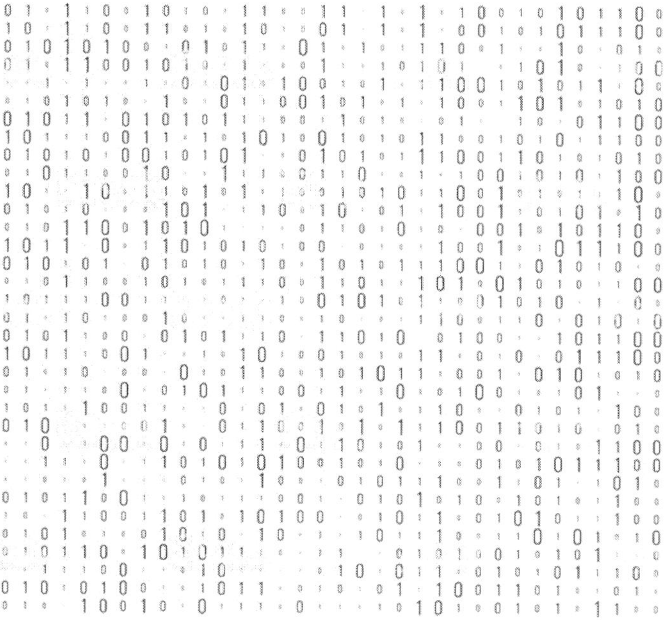

8

Iron Condor

An options strategy created with four options contracts in the hopes to take advantage of low volatility.

The safe house was empty. “What do we do?” I asked.

Agent Marron was at a loss. “This wasn’t the way it was supposed to go down, Kyle.”

Chrystle explained to me that Drew was going to be my handler through all of this; a person that I'd come to trust, at the very least. "We wanted that connection because what I was going to tell the two of you would absolutely blow your minds."

There was a sound of creaking wood. Marron grabbed me and ushered me back to the car. She quickly turned the key in the ignition and slammed on the gas, getting us out of there in a hurry. "My priority right now is to get you to a safe spot, Kyle. I didn't want this to be how you learned about everything."

Chrystle went into defensive driving mode. After what seemed like an hour, maybe longer, she finally pulled off the road, onto a dirt path. We weren't on the path very long before a rather ominous building came into view. It looked like something out of a nineteen seventies movie about the Russians nuking us. It was four cement walls with a heavy looking door on the front side, a satellite dish fixed to the roof, and no windows from what I could tell. Once parked and out of the car, Agent Marron walked over and looked at a little scanner off to the side. A second later, the door opened, allowing us entry.

"Follow me, we have some important people waiting for us."

We went down a set of iron stairs into the basement. There, it was clear this was some sort of secret location, as there were modern computers, screens, and a small armory waiting for us. Chrystle and I were the only people here, however.

"I thought you said people were waiting to meet us?"

"Turn around."

The large monitor behind came to life, throwing us into a Zoom meeting. Four figures were on-screen, looking down towards the spot Agent Marron and I stood. "Kyle Carlisle, welcome to the Department of Arcane Research and Knowledge."

"Or," the man on the top left corner spoke up, "as we call it, DARK."

"Kyle, allow me to introduce you to the officers of DARK. You just met former Navy SEAL Captain George Parkers. Next, in clockwise rotation, we have aerospace engineer Doctor Ryan Jameson, and finally, we have CIA Agent J. Charles Lattrell. The only person missing from our small operation is Director Keith Herbert and he should be arriving any minute now."

Sure enough, just as she finished the introductions, an older gentleman with snowy white hair and a full beard entered the basement headquarters. He was wearing a black suit and an expression of disgust on his face. "Damnit, losing Muldoon was a blow. Do we know how it happened, Special Agent Marron?"

"Gunshot wounds, sir. It looked like he was ambushed. Whoever pulled that off was long gone by the time I arrived with Mister Carlisle."

Herbert extended his hand. "A pleasure to meet you, son. I didn't want it to be under circumstances like this, but it seems we are behind the eight ball yet again."

"Sir, with all due respect," Captain Parkers interrupted. "If you had allowed me to assemble a team and hit War Dog Labs before the FBI got involved, we could've been out in front."

"Hindsight is twenty-twenty, Parkers." Herbert returned his gaze to me. "Mister Carlisle, you are in quite a spot, not knowing what in God's name is going on and being whisked away to some top-secret black ops site ran by a shadow organization within the US government."

That was a lot to digest.

"Long story short is DARK investigates threats to the United States that can't be quantified. We've looked into both demonic and extraterrestrial threats that would make the manliest of men cry. To date, we've had a one hundred percent success rate in neutralizing threats, until now," he added.

"Can someone please tell me what's happening?" I asked.

"We're hoping whatever Agent Muldoon had you steal off the Pandemos girl's laptop can tell all of us what's happening," Herbert replied.

I fished around in my pocket and pulled out the USB. As soon as he had his hands on it, he placed it into the central computer, which flashed up on another screen adjacent to the Zoom meeting. This was the moment we were all waiting for, to see what juicy information we were able to get from Amy and prove she was some sort of villainous mastermind.

Except nothing flashed up.

Well, a bunch of cat memes did, but nothing else.

"My career and good name were put on the line for cat memes?" My question had started as a low grumble before it crescendoed into practically yelling. "To think I actually believed this whole act of how one lady could potentially be some sort of monster, or at the very least, just a bad lady. DARK, c'mon guys, give me a break."

It felt really good to get that off of my chest.

None of the men said anything. Director Herbert seemed particularly blanched by my over the top rebuttal. It was up to Agent Marron to pick up the pieces. "There's a chance that this is encrypted, Kyle. Can you give us a chance?"

"A chance? Chrystle, these are cat memes for crying out loud!"

"She might be right, Kyle," the scientist guy Doctor Jameson agreed.

"Lattrell, does the CIA have anyone we can use?" Herbert asked.

"No one I trust," the spook answered. "What about the Navy, Parkers?"

"I've been away too long. If I asked for a favor now, it'd be suspicious."

These guys were turning out to be less than useful. "If no one has any great suggestions, can I go home now? I've got things to do tomorrow."

"There is one guy we can reach out to," Marron suggested.

Everyone, in the room and via Zoom directed their attention towards Director Herbert. The tension became so thick, as if this had been a conversation that had been aired out before. "We don't even know if this hacker exists. You want to go on a wild goose chase with something this important?"

"Does anyone else have any ideas?"

I assumed hackers were a dime a dozen. "What makes this one so special?"

Chrystle hooked her arm around mine. "Gentlemen, I think this meeting is adjourned for the night. I'm taking Kyle home."

Before we could leave, "Mister Carlisle, I hope we can count on you in the future, if needed," Director Herbert said to me.

I didn't respond as Chrystle took me from the DARK basement and back out to her car. As we pulled away, "This night brought less clarity than I expected, Agent Marron."

"Please, it's Chrystle. The Agent Marron stuff makes me feel old."

"I wanted answers and we got cat memes. Is there anything you can tell me that you wouldn't have before?"

That's when Chrystle unloaded a story on me that defied logic. After she inserted herself into the FBI as Agent Muldoon's new partner, the two of them went back to War Dog Labs. There, they found a man chained up on the third level, the same symbol that was on RedKoin etched in the wall behind him. The man gave the two of them a few lines about being a higher power than humans before dying… disappearing into nothingness. That's when Marron knew this was something more than just a dead end or hunch that DARK didn't need to investigate further. It was in that moment she knew something very deadly was upon them.

"It leads back to two things," she went on. "War Dog Labs had two projects going on at the time Agents Muldoon and Schulte raided them; the Aphrodite Paradox and the Hades Pathogen. Both Drew and I were hoping whatever you got off of Amy Pandemos' computer would've given us the intelligence we needed to take our next steps."

I understood her disappointment now. “Devil’s advocate here, but the fact that we found nothing, doesn’t that just prove Amy’s innocence?”

“Have you heard of a gang called the Titans, Kyle?”

That felt like an odd question. “No, though gangs aren’t really my thing.”

“The hacker I’ve been trying to locate, for years now, is a member of that gang, or so I’m inclined to believe. He goes by Kronos and he’s been in communication with me a few times in the past. If we can find him, maybe he can sort this out once and for all. Is Miss Pandemos a threat or just a motivated woman with a lot of money?”

That gave me a lot to think on the rest of the drive back to my apartment. The one image that kept coming back to haunt me was the death of Agent Muldoon. It bothered me that no one at DARK even acknowledged the fact the man was dead, for reasons we didn’t even know. When I brought that up, Chrystle didn’t even have to say a word; her reaction spoke volumes.

It was only when we pulled up outside of my apartment that, she give me something to go on. “Kyle, this is a dangerous time. Something big is happening and we don’t even know what, yet. Please, do me a favor and be careful, okay?”

****

It was early when my phone rang. I was hoping to pretty much sleep all day after all the crazy stuff that had happened last night. "Hello," I answered groggily.

"Kyle." Oh man, it was Amy. "Care to meet me at the Bagel King in thirty? I thought I'd treat you to breakfast."

"Of course, give me a few extra to get ready."

I didn't have a very good feeling about this. Actually, the last thing Agent Marron asked me to do was to be careful. Going to breakfast with my boss, who this weird government organization thinks is the devil or something, actually made me feel good. This was a chance to get back to normal. In my mind, I broke into her office and the only thing we found were cat memes. It was painfully obvious that Amy was just a smart businesswoman and people were always out to get smart business women.

It didn't take long to shower, get dressed, and head out the door. By the time I pulled into the Bagel King's parking lot, quite a few people were waiting around to get a table. As I walked in, Amy was already seated with a coffee. She waved for me to come join her and immediately a waiter approached, even before I had a chance to sit down.

"What may I get you, sir?" he asked, as I was trying to slide into the booth.

"Can I get a cherry coke and a glass of water?"

"Certainly." With that, he walked quickly behind the counter, getting my drinks and paying no attention to anyone else."

"People sure do like you," I said, noticing how no one else got that sort of treatment.

"It helps when you own the place."

My continued education of my new boss continued. She had apparently been working behind the scenes at Ares Commerce for a long time before she took an interest in GenX and used her built up war chest to purchase them outright. The moment she did, she sent them public and, as we already established, it failed miserably. That was when she found out about War Dog Labs and how they were stealing projects from her from insiders who wanted her to fail.

"The FBI took care of that problem for me, one of the few things they've done right."

I wasn't sure if I should say anything, but what the hell. I needed to gauge Amy's reaction, to see if there was any chance she was involved in anything shady... or even paranormal? "Did you hear that FBI agent who talked to me actually died last night?"

"I read that in the paper this morning. I can't say I liked what he was trying to do to you, but I highly doubt he deserved to die. He was the one who solved the War Dog Labs case for me."

Her answer actually satisfied my curiosity. In fact, I was once again questioning myself as to how I let myself get caught up in this insanity. The rest of breakfast was quite nice as Amy explained how her team of computer engineers were mining the blockchains, gathering more and more RedKoin to begin selling to the masses.

And that's where I was going to come in.

"I'm going to give you the tools, Kyle, to get RedKoin into as many hands as possible. I am even open to selling partial coins. If someone can only afford a quarter of a coin, so be it," Amy said, with glee in her voice. "We are going to break down walls, get this amazing investment into the hands of people who never thought investing was possible."

"People like me, the guys and girls who were born on the wrong side of the tracks."

"Exactly! Why should cryptocurrency only be for the rich or the shady? RedKoin is a legit crypto that can be used in stores, making purchases on the internet, even gifting to a family member for educational purposes. Where the American dollar is failing, RedKoin will be there to pick up the slack."

I almost wanted to stand up and give her a standing ovation. "How do we make this happen?" I asked.

"Simple - we get people to stop buying from brokerage firms like Global Options and buy directly from us."

There was an old practice by brokerage firms that sold cryptocurrency to their clients that the firm actually owned the coins and the customers were given rights to the gains or losses from the coins. In essence, if you bought the coins from a brokerage firm, you were basically leasing the coins until you sold them back, at either a profit or a loss. However, if a person bought them on their own, through a banking app or one of those cash accounts, you actually bought and held the coin in your own name. If you did that, not only did you get the gains or losses, but you had very real currency to spend. For a lot of people, ownership was still a big deal.

If we could market it like that, I thought, we'd open ourselves up to a bigger, broader audience.

"We need to promote the value of ownership. People need to understand the fundamental difference between having rights to RedKoin and actually owning it. Besides, GenX would get a bigger piece of the profits, correct?" I asked.

"Getting more money into GenX is just what I need, too. You're going to be a real asset, Kyle."

Amy held up her glass and we clinked our drinks together. "To new, very profitable partnerships," she toasted.

"I can drink to that!"

9

Red Herring

A preliminary prospectus filed by a company with regulators, usually in connection with the company's initial public offering.

My third day on the job and we were already making monumental strides in the sale of RedKoin. The first thing I did was to create www.redkoin.com. It was an interactive site that showed just how many coins were currently in circulation, how many were for sale, and the estimated next batch. It also included current bid and ask prices, as well as a currency exchange, which showed the different values of RedKoin depending on which country a person lived in.

Just from having the website up and having people buying and selling directly with us, our bottom line was already gaining some serious weight.

"The feedback is pouring in," Amy told me as she poured some scotch into glasses. "Our RedKoin website is exactly what crypto traders have been looking for."

"Just you wait until the social media pages go live tomorrow. Just think, dedicated groups just to buy and sell RedKoin and the strategies they use. You thought you had something before - RedKoin is going to take off to the moon and back," I promised.

"Can you add something else to the website?" she asked.

"Of course. Making changes is pretty simple; what do you have in mind?"

"I'd love for a project countdown placed on the website, so people can see what their investments in RedKoin are going towards and how soon they can expect to see results."

This was a topic that I very much wanted to probe about, but always felt it wasn't really my place. "That's not a problem. But," I went on, "do you think I can get some inside info on these projects I've heard so much about?"

She stood up and motioned for me to follow. "The scientists at GenX are pretty protective of their research, but since no one else is here, shall we?"

Amy took me down the stairs into the main lobby and then off to the right. She punched in a seven to eight-digit key code and the door swung backwards. From there, we went down another hallway before coming to a second security door. There, she performed an eye scan and a fingerprint before that door allowed us entry. When she said protective of their research, Amy wasn't lying.

Behind the second door was a wide open, spacious laboratory. Desks, computers, whiteboards, test tubes, everything you'd expect to see and more were scattered around the large room. "Welcome to the first war room, where the project affectionately known as the Aphrodite Paradox is taking shape."

There was so much to take in. "What exactly is happening here?"

She picked up one of the binders on the table nearest to where we were standing, "Did you ever wonder what goes on inside a coma patient's mind?" she asked suddenly.

"As sad as it sounds, not really."

"We can see the body, but the mind, does it disappear? Does it move on, only to come back?" Amy was getting really deep, fast. "The team here is working on finding out what happens to the mind once the body stops, but isn't dead."

"That sounds like an amazing use of science, but I don't quite understand the name," I admitted.

"Aphrodite was the Greek goddess of beauty and, as the saying goes, the mind is a beautiful thing. Just a play on words, Kyle."

I didn't quite feel so dumb after that explanation.

We walked all the way to the back of the lab where yet another security door was waiting. This one needed a security card and a retina scan open. This lab wasn't nearly as open or as bright as the last one we'd just left. This one felt... evil. Like something that was going on here could potentially be what Agent Muldoon or maybe even Chrystle were after. I stood near the door, as the chill in the air was very unsettling.

"Amy, what's going on here?"

"This is the home to the Hades Pathogen project."

As soon as the words rolled off of her tongue, something inside of me began to churn. I almost felt like I could be sick.

"Are you okay, Kyle?"

"Maybe I ate something that disagreed with me earlier," I responded. Sweat began to bead around my hairline.

She pulled up a chair and guided me into the seat. "You've also been working like a fool since you started on Monday. You might have just pushed yourself too hard. Why don't you take tomorrow off?" Amy offered.

"No, I don't want to take a sick day three days in," I protested.

"You've worked harder in three days than some people under me have in a year. No, it's not a sick day, it's a scheduled rest day, fully paid."

This seemed like a conversation I was going to lose. "If you say so, boss," I relented.

"I do." Amy grabbed a chair and sat down too. "While we wait for you to feel a bit better, let me tell you what happens here. We are trying to create a base vaccine."

"A base vaccine - what's that?"

"It would be the base compound that could be used to produce multiple vaccines for multiple different viruses. Do you know how this could change the bio-tech game? One base vaccine that we could formulate and change depending on the situation."

"When you said you were out to change the world, you weren't joking, Amy."

"I don't joke about a better future. With what you're doing, the monumental effort with RedKoin, we will have more money than we need to finish these projects off, and soon."

Whatever had caused me to feel sick slowly faded away. As I stood up, "Thank you for letting me know what you're working on. It means a lot."

"You don't understand, Kyle; this is what we're working on."

Eventually we made our way back out to the lobby where we said our goodnights. I was dog tired when I got home and could only think about getting out of my suit and falling asleep. Lady Luck wasn't on my side. Sitting on my couch was one Chrystle Marron. "Home late tonight, Kyle," she said casually.

"How did you get in here?"

"Please, I'm a federal agent. Picking a lock to an apartment complex is child's play."

"Fair point," I said, respectfully. "But why are you here?"

Her tone went from casual to excited, just like that. "Kronos is willing to meet and crack open the USB, on two conditions."

There was a word no one liked - conditions. “What are they, Chrystle?”

“Apparently this hacker knows about some of the artifacts that DARK has collected over the years. The first condition is that I liberate a scythe from the underground vault and bring it to him. And that’s where the second condition comes in, that you participate and come with me to meet him.”

“No thanks,” I answered, plainly.

“I figured you weren’t interested since you haven't responded to any of my messages, but I have little choice in the matter. Kronos said you need to come along and that the adventure would make sense only to you. I have no idea what that means,” she pleaded. “I need you for this, Kyle.”

“If I do this and we find nothing, I want a promise that DARK and the FBI will back off of Amy and her corporations.”

“Deal.”

“Just like that?” I asked.

“Considering this is my investigation, I can pretty much call it off when I feel its resolved itself. If we find nothing, I’ll call it off,” she proposed.

“Then what do we need to do?”

The plan was far from simple. Tomorrow afternoon, DARK was hosting an investor’s event under the guise as a subsidiary of the FBI. Chrystle wanted me to come as her date to the event. For about an hour, we'd have to walk around and talk to the guests. Once Director Herbert began his speech, we'd have our window of opportunity.

"Even though DARK is a very small agency, we have protection. If there was an active mission, Parkers would have a squad together composed of SEALs, rangers, and two CIA handlers. Luckily, there is no ongoing mission. The only thing we'll have to worry about are the Blackstone operators that Herbert keeps on retention. They are highly trained private security; however, they tend to be a bit lax in certain situations. Allow me to take care of that."

That was a whole lot of information at once, but I rolled with it. "I wonder what's so important about this scythe?"

Chrystle pulled a tablet out of her bag and began typing. As soon as she found what she was looking for, she turned the screen towards me. "It is either Roman or Greek in nature, made from bronze. It appears to be a weapon of some sort, probably for a specialized soldier. Most warriors of that time period used a type of sword or a spear."

I studied the scythe closely. I'd never seen it before, that I knew, but there was something oddly familiar about it. "What time do we need to leave tomorrow? Is there a dress code?"

"Kyle, I think we need to be careful. Amy Pandemos is one of our suspects in the death of Drew Muldoon. I can't just have you skipping work for no reason."

"She gave me the day off ironically enough. I got a bit sick tonight, probably from eating crappy food and working too hard the past few days."

Chrystle raised an eyebrow in response, but pushed no further. "In that case," she went on, "I'll pick you up here at three. The event starts at four and its business casual. A polo shirt and nice pants should be just fine."

"I've worked with Amy for the last three days; I'm telling you she seems like a legit businesswoman. I hope you'll believe me on this one," I said.

"I want to, I really do. Trust me, I want nothing more than for everyone I cross paths with to be a good person who really wants to change the world. But, Kyle," she went on, her voice growing stern, "I need you to understand something is happening, something I'm afraid may be very evil and malicious."

When she said the world evil, it brought me right back to the lab where the Hades Pathogen project was taking place. I hadn't and wasn't going to tell Chrystle about those projects, as they were shown to me in confidence and I didn't want to add any fuel to the speculative fire. So, I just shook my head and pretended to understand what she was saying.

"Can I ask what happened to make you sick?"

"I told you, over working and poor eating habits."

I could tell she didn't believe me. Hell, I didn't really believe it myself.

That's when there was a knock on the door. "I'm not expecting anyone," I said, anxiously.

"I took the liberty to order pizza for us. I hope that's okay."

No man says no to pizza, me included. I grabbed a few beers from the fridge and the two of us began to dig in. It was Hawaiian style, not my favorite, but it was also free, which was my favorite. I felt there was one last motive with Chrystle still being here, the pizza being a red herring. By the time I was on my third slice, another truth began to shine through.

"One of the things they drill into our heads at Quantico is never get attached to a mission, or the players in the mission. I'm trying my best, Kyle, but this one's not easy."

"How so?"

"I'm going to lay it all out for you. The first time we met, I felt a bit of a spark. It could very well just be the lonely life of a DARK agent, or maybe there was something there on your end. I don't really know," she rambled on.

"It's not just you, Chrystle. There's something, I'll admit it, but I don't know if it's such a good idea. Maybe your Quantico training is the right way to go - at least while all this nonsense is happening," I added.

"You're right, of course. I'm just glad to know it wasn't just me."

We finished up and Chrystle went to leave. "Tomorrow at three, okay? I'll get you through this, but I need you to trust me every step of the way."

"Yes ma'am."

"I'll see you then." She leaned over and gave me a kiss on the cheek.

That last interaction stayed with me the remainder of the night as sleep didn't really come my way.

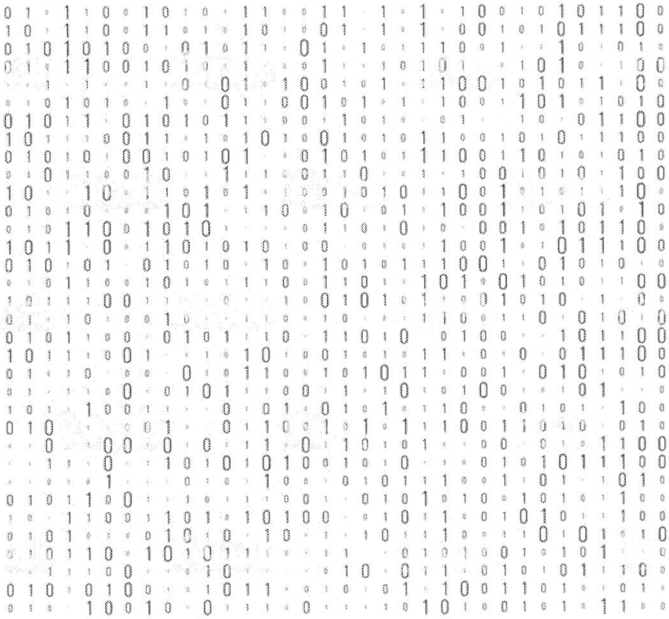

10

Futures

An auction market in which participants buy and sell commodity and futures contracts for delivery on a specified future date.

"Where are you, Agent Marron?"

The minute I got back into my car, Herbert was already up my ass. "I'm driving home, Director," I answered sharply.

His voice continued to insert itself over my car's speakers. "I'm not sure what you're up to right now, but that situation I instructed you to deal with still hasn't been dealt with. The higher ups are-"

"Sir," I cut him off, "I'm looking into Kronos. I've got a solid lead on him and, if all goes well, the USB will be in his hands tomorrow evening for encryption."

"That's all fine and well," he retorted. "We have a dead FBI agent in a case involving DARK. I need closure in that death so I can get those suits off of our business."

Pushing me about Agent Muldoon's death was a bad choice. "What would you have me do, sir? We have one flimsy lead and if I arrest her, her army of lawyers will fight it and win, I can assure you of that."

"We need a headline, Marron. Get me one."

With that, the call disconnected and my perfectly good mood was ruined. It was late, my emotions were already conflicted over what transpired with Kyle, and the only lead I had was a USB full of cat memes. How in the hell was I supposed to produce some magical future headline when we had next to nothing? It was like Herbert wanted me to become a private investigator and spy on Amy Pandemos.

Actually, I was pretty sure that was exactly what he wanted me to do.

My townhouse was on the edge of the west side of the city, however, I did a U-turn and proceeded back towards GenX. I was conflicted with the order; there was already too many hiccups that had gone down that I was dealing with internally. I was being pulled in two different directions, yet I knew that getting Herbert something would satisfy his need to get his *headline*. The man was so vain sometimes that it was almost too easy to do what needed to be done while keeping him in the dark.

I chuckled at my own little joke.

Gods above, I was turning into my father, rest his soul.

As I was driving, my mind drifted back to my last assignment before this one. I'd been deployed to Puerto Rico where kids were mysteriously disappearing. Once the usual suspects - drug cartels, sex traffickers, and the like were cleared, DARK got the call and Herbert sent me to do what I do best. I wasn't even in Puerto Rico forty-eight hours when I discovered something so sinister that even I wasn't prepared.

It turned out Puerto Rico was home to an insane cult of cannibals. Not just any cannibals, mind you, but ones who preferred children. It was with great pleasure that I sent the evidence back to Herbert and ordered a drone strike on the mountain stronghold in which they called home. One did survive and I was able to interrogate him. He claimed they were instructed by their master, Satan, to release the children from their human prisons so that Satan could collect their souls for his army of the damned.

That case still haunted my nightmares to this day.

That was the day I knew I needed to seek my own ace in the hole.

Across the street from GenX was a French bistro. I pulled around back, as the restaurant was closed and I wanted to make sure I was parked in a blind spot to any cameras they may have had set up for security. Once I found the right spot, I pulled in and took a few moments to formulate a plan. I needed to be careful to make sure I didn't trip any alarms or tip off any security guards. This needed to be a clean mission, to ensure all parties were satisfied with the results.

I had the skill to do so, but a little luck couldn't hurt, either.

Good thing for me that I had a friend back in DC who specialized in luck.

I put my earpiece in and dialed his number. He was a bit of a night owl, so I crossed my fingers and hoped for the best.

On the third ring, "Good lord, Chrystle Marron, do you know what time it is here?"

"Yes, I do, Eric Woodfield," I answered, using his full name for the same snarky effect he was going for.

Eric had made his name back in the early nineties assisting FBI agents with a string of very odd shark attack cases. All of those files were sealed; God above knows I would've loved to have seen what was in those. The real reason for my call was Eric was an exceptional ally when it came to technology. Part of me wanted to ask him if he could hack the USB currently tucked away in my jacket pocket, but if he did, he'd have to report everything. If Kronos was the one to do it, the information was mine. With that came the ability to share it at my choosing.

Back to the conversation at hand, "I need to break into the address I just texted you. Let me know if you can assist."

To know Eric was to know he loved to grumble about everything. "Oh damn, girl! You want me to break into GenX's security system to get you in?"

"Just a little midnight fun, right, Eric?"

I began to hear the clacking of keys in the receiver. I took that as a win; we'd soon gain access to the building. "You owe me, Chrystle," Eric muttered as he typed.

"This isn't too hard for you, is it?"

"Please, the only hiccup is whoever installed this system knew what they were doing. It's an up-to-date fiber optic system that uses analog codes to keep people like me out. Fortunately for you, Ms. Marron, I am the absolute best at what I do."

"That's the reason I called."

There was a half snort, half cough on the other end. "You should be golden. The camera system inside will play a feed that I've uploaded, masking your presence. I even took the liberty to knock out the traffic cams in the area. That should give you about an hour or so, before they are back up. As for the guards inside, I assume you can handle them on your own?" he asked.

"I'll be fine from here on out."

"Good, call me later. I want to hear all about this."

I kept my earpiece in, just in case. I got out of my car and jogged across the street, my hood up. I'd already picked my access point, which was the backdoor along the south side of the building. As suspected, the door had a keypad lock to prevent entry. My faith in Eric was about to be tested; I grabbed the handle and pulled. The door opened freely, granting me access. Nothing like a bit of illegal hacking to go along with an illegal search.

It didn't take me long to run into my first guard. The larger man in black Kevlar with a standard issued Berretta never saw me coming. I quickly struck him in the back of the head and he dropped to the ground. This was a stealth mission; keep the guard interactions to a minimum and get out fast.

That's when the earpiece began to buzz. I looked around before I answered. "Hello?" I answered in a whisper.

"Girl, I couldn't let you do this on your own."

"Eric?"

"Listen, I was able to pull schematics of the building. I don't know what you're up to, but Talia would kill me if I didn't help you," he explained.

Talia Bordeaux was my training agent at Quantico. She was the one who opened my eyes to the fact that this world was full of secrets and wonder. "I don't know what I'd do without you."

"It's a damn shame you left the bureau for whatever clandestine operation you're in now."

Leaving the FBI for DARK had been the toughest decision I ever made. When Director Herbert came to me about this team and the objectives he had, there was no way I could've said no. And then when I started my work here, it became so much more than I ever expected. A tough decision, yes, but one I'd make again without hesitation.

"It looks like if you take this back hallway, it'll lead you around to a few areas that are just labeled as containment - high risk. Are you trying to see what GenX is up to?"

As juicy as that sounded, I didn't have time to do any extra snooping. No, it was important to stay on task. "I'm trying to see if Amy Pandemos has anything to do with the death of Drew Muldoon. I'm looking for her office."

"Hmmmm," Eric hummed. "Drew's death has some of the brass here shaken up, too. According to his field office, he hadn't been acting like himself the day before."

"Something spooked him, that's for sure," I agreed, leaving out the juicy stuff.

"Pandemos' office is around the front, at the top of the stairs. You'll probably have to beat a few guys down along the way," he warned me.

Eric fed me the directions to get to my target. I desperately didn't want to get into any shootout situations or three, four against one spots. Taking my time, I checked each corner before I rounded it and stayed as low as I could. People tended not to focus either above or below. Using basic human psychology to my advantage had worked for me before; I crossed my fingers that whoever Pandemos hired here were just as susceptible.

The main lobby was in front of me. There were two security agents stationed in the middle and another one at the top of the stairs. Here came the real test. "Any other ways, Eric?"

"The building has only two floors and there's no elevator. Most of the actual first floor is barricaded off. Even though the security system is under my control, none of those routes lead to Pandemos' office. If you want to get to her secrets, the lobby is options A, B, and C."

It was time to see what alternatives I had. The second floor seemed to be more of an overhang to the first floor than an actual dedicated floor. Above me was the exposed underside; there were rafters and HVAC lines running that if I could reach, I could use to get around the guards. With one problem solved, another presented itself. How did I get up there?

"Eric, above me is-"

"I'm already on it. There is a maintenance crawl space in that overhead section. The problem is getting to it. There is a ladder hidden in a closet behind the front desk. If you can get there, we can get you into Pandemos' office pretty easily."

Okay, I could do this. I wouldn't need to go too far into the lobby to get behind the desk; I just needed to be fast about it. I moved into position and gave one last look at the task in front of me. Both guards were chatting, looking towards the front doors. Stay low, I reminded myself, and don't stop moving. With my window open now, I crouched down and beelined it towards the desk. I refused to look up, for what I couldn't see couldn't hurt me. The moment I knew I was behind the desk, I pushed myself under the wooden table and took a few deep breaths to calm myself. There was no angry yelling or footsteps coming towards me. I'd made it. Now, I needed to open the door and get to the ladder.

"You catch the game last night?" I heard one of the guards ask.

"Yeah, I lost a ton of money on it."

Good, they were talking and occupied. I crept out and slowly opened the closet door. I didn't need to open it much and was able to get in, closing it behind me. Phew - I was sweating from all the stress and tension. As I climbed up the ladder, "Didn't expect it to go that well," I whispered.

"We're not out of the woods yet. You still have to leave afterwards."

It was very easy from here to sneak in through the floor register into Amy's office. Eric continued his remote guidance, leading me to the right return vent. Once I was in the office, the real search began. It became evident not too far into my search that there was going to be little, if anything, incriminating here, as I suspected. Amy would want to make someone who broke into her office work for clues, if she had left any at all. I smiled to myself, as this felt like a potential scavenger hunt, if I had the patience to play. Unfortunately, I was tired and I didn't want to be doing this to start with.

Another time, perhaps.

The last place I checked was her desk. Again, nothing that outright said she was behind the murder of Agent Muldoon. I was about to give up and began heading back when I found something of interest. "Eric, I think I found an FBI ID card. A lot of the information has been scrubbed off of it, but it looks like the ID number is still legible. Can you run it for me?"

"Let me know when you're ready."

I rattled off the number and waited. I wasn't expecting Eric's gasp on the other end. "That card belonged to deceased Agent Rebecca Schulte. Wasn't she…?"

"Drew Muldoon's partner? Yes, she was." Oh, the irony of the situation. "Are there any notes on her, Eric?"

"The actual details of her death are completely redacted. However, I do have her background information, if you'd like it," he offered.

He had quite the backstory to share on Agent Schulte. She was an orphan, finally adopted at age thirteen. At age sixteen, her adopted parents died in a home invasion gone wrong. Schulte had been shot herself and by all accounts, should've died. She somehow survived and went on to get a Bright Futures scholarship for a full ride, studying finance. It was in her senior year that the FBI came calling, in the form of Agent Talia Bordeaux. Schulte actually had turned her down and repeatedly said no until she was finally persuaded by Congresswoman Pamela Garrison.

"Her death was taken pretty hard back here in DC. She was a bright star, both in the bureau and in the political field. God," he went on, "they scrubbed her file completely. I don't even have a picture to send you."

Herbert wouldn't be able to use this for any sort of grand jury indictment, but it would be enough for him to get his pats on the back and even more marching orders from those above him. I privately thanked Amy for the red herring.

"Eric, I think I've stayed long enough. Let's get out of here."

No sooner did I close the drawer than the office door flew open; two men standing there with their guns pointed at me. "Don't move and we won't shoot."

"Eric, I need to call you back."

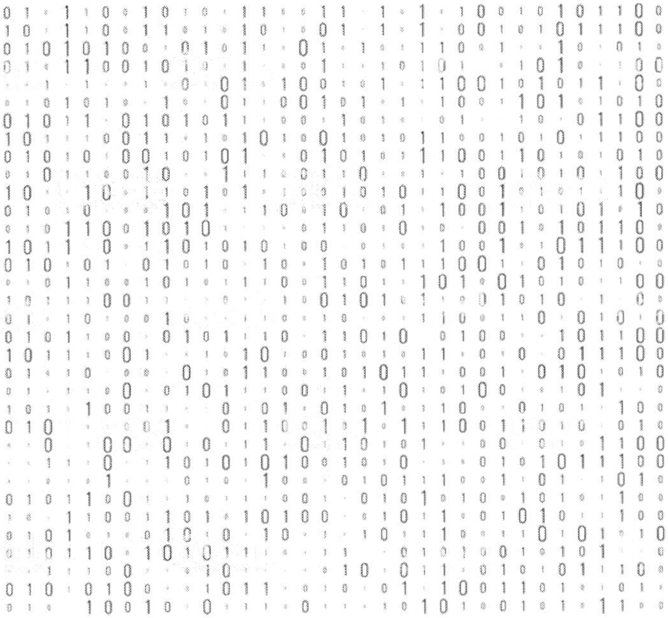

11

Circuit Breaker

A temporarily halt in trading on an exchange, which are in place to curb panic-selling.

"Hello?" I answered groggily.

"Kyle, no one else has answered. I need your help."

The voice on the other end was calm at first, but some panic was creeping in. That broke me out of my fog. “Chrystle, is that you?”

“I’m not going to get into much over the phone, but I’ve already had to put down two hostile targets and I’ve been wounded myself. My car’s been compromised and I really need a ride back to DARK. Can you help me?” she asked.

“I’m dreaming right?”

“Kyle!” she whispered urgently into the phone. “I’m at the corner of Maple and Dixon. If you can help, I really could use some.”

I wasn’t about to leave her bleeding on the street somewhere. “I’m on my way,” I said.

The streets she gave me sounded familiar to me, and when I got there, I figured out why. She was two streets over from GenX. I opened my car door and Chrystle slumped into the car. “Are you going to be okay?”

“Yeah,” she answered through gritted teeth. “It’s more painful than life threatening,” she told me.

“Can you get me to the DARK facility?”

“I can. Turn left here,” she instructed right away.

My hands were gripped tight around the steering wheel. “What the hell happened? Are there people still after you?”

“I don’t think so. You picked me up in record time and... ohhh that hurts. Anyways, I think we’re in the clear.”

“You avoided the question about what you were doing?” I asked again as I merged onto the highway.

Chrystle wasn’t making eye contact with me. “I was inside GenX. Director Herbert ordered me to do an illegal search to see if I could find anything that connected Amy Pandemos to the death of Agent Drew Muldoon.”

“You what?!”

“Can you give me the third degree later? I mean, my God, I’ve been shot and none of my DARK contacts even picked up the phone or responded to my emergency text codes.”

Wow - talk about loyalty. I was about to say something else, but stopped. It seemed like a good time to let things chill for a minute or two before we re-engaged in the conversation. I could tell she was in a ton of pain, anyways. “There’s pain killers in the glove box,” I offered.

“Thanks.”

As Chrystle took two with no water, I looked in the rearview mirror. Headlights from a truck behind us seemed to be getting awfully close to my car. I started to speed up, but so did the truck. This gave me pause for concern. “I think we’re being tailed, Chrystle.”

"Crap," she agreed. "Kyle, you're about to get rammed."

Her intuition was spot on. The truck sped up quicker than I could and crashed into the back of my car. The impact sent both of us forward for a second before the seatbelt locked and whipped us back into the seat. Not wanting to experience that again, I pulled into the left-hand lane and pushed the accelerator down as far as it could go.

"That truck's faster than us," Chrystle observed.

Our pursuers didn't follow us. Instead, they stayed in the right lane and tried to get up alongside us. Luck was on our side as the highway split into three lanes. As soon as it did, I swung out left again, giving us some distance.

Crack!

Crack!

"Are they shooting at us?"

"Poorly, but yes they are. Hang on a second, we'll even the playing field."

Chrystle dug around and pulled out her own handgun. Rolling down the window, she took two shots at the truck, hitting the tires and sending it off the road. The driver lost control at that point and the vehicle went into a spin before buckling over and rolling out of sight. It was like a scene from an action movie. Thank God no one saw us. I just kept driving, my foot frozen on the gas pedal.

"Are you okay, Kyle?"

"Hell no I'm not okay, but there's little else for me to do except get you to DARK."

She tucked her gun back into her holster, grimacing the entire time. Then she pulled out her phone and brought a picture up. "This here," she showed me. "This is the ID to Agent Rebecca Schulte. She was Drew Muldoon's partner until she died the night the two of them raided War Dog Labs. Now," she stopped for a moment, grabbing her side, "This isn't proof that Amy Pandemos killed Muldoon, but why does your boss have the FBI ID card to a dead agent?"

That was a good question.

One I didn't have an answer for.

"I'm not defending her," I said, slowly. "And I get that looks bad, but couldn't there be another explanation for her having that?"

"I don't know," Chrystle responded. "Let's just add that to the list of weird things going on, and they all seemed to be centered around GenX."

We finally pulled up to the old building that I'd come to understand as a front. I got her out of the car and helped her inside. I had to lend a hand to gain us access to DARK's main facility, downstairs. No one else was there currently, which made me curious as to why I didn't take her to the emergency room or at least an all-night clinic. Chrystle made her way to a part of the room that I hadn't been to yet. She sat down in a chair and dosed herself with something. Then she began the awful actions of pulling a bullet out of her shoulder by herself.

"Do you need any help?" I asked, a bit squeamish.

"No, I've had to do this a time or two. You get used to the pain."

"I'm beginning to wonder if you're not the one we should be worried about. I'm not entirely sure you're human," I joked.

With a set of tweezers, she yanked the bullet free. There was a decent amount of blood still coming out of the wound. I gave her a thick gauze pad, which she pressed against it. "I'm going to have to stitch this up."

"You're definitely going to need help with that."

She winced but didn't disagree. To be clear, I had no idea what I was doing, but I had some sewing experience from a home economics class I took in high school. That'd been a long time ago, but I still remembered the basics. I threaded the needle with the string and tied a knot around the loose end, holding it in place. With the thread ready, I pulled on some gloves and got to work. I kept a mental image that these were just two pieces of fabric that needed to be sewn back together. I did my best to block out the blood and Chrystle's soft moans of pain.

"Tell me something," she panted. "Anything useless or weird, to help keep my mind off you stitching up a bullet wound."

"When most people hear the term circuit breaker, they think of the panel in their homes. For me, I think of a market halt. Strange, I know, but it can either make you a lot of money if you know how to work it or you can go broke before you even have a chance to blink." I'm not sure why I went with circuit breaker, but Chrystle's attention was on me and not the stitches. "A circuit breaker lasts as few as seven minutes. Just think about that, you could lose almost everything in less time than it takes most people to run a mile."

"To get into the FBI, I had to run a four-and-a-half-minute mile. I know it's another useless fact, but the bureau wants people who can hopefully outrun a gunshot coming their way."

I thought back on the last market-wide circuit breaker I dealt with. I'd just started at Global Options. "In the moment, when stuff like that's going on, time seems to slow down, like it's never going to end."

"Yet, when you look back at it, the memory speeds it up into real time, like it's just a blip on the radar."

I'm not entirely sure what happened at that moment. I'd just finished a pretty horrible stitch job as Chrystle leaned in and kissed me. I didn't back away; no, I returned the favor tenfold. Maybe it'd been the adrenaline of everything that'd happened, or maybe this was a continuation of events that took place at my apartment before she left. God, that'd seemed like weeks ago, not just hours ago.

I finally broke away. "I still don't think we should be doing this."

"I don't either."

But we continued anyway.

****

It was a little after four thirty in the morning when I woke up on the Murphy bed that Chrystle and I finally had fallen asleep on about an hour or so earlier. She was still very much asleep. Good, I thought. She needed rest after being shot and everything that happened. I gathered up my clothes, got dressed, and snuck out of DARK as quietly as I could. The moon was still high in the sky, illuminating everything with the brightness it was stealing from the sun. I pushed everything out of my mind, staying calm and collected as I drove home.

It was only when I was back on the highway did I begin to feel everything that had happened. As I was passing the spot where Chrystle had shot the tires of the truck, I saw the police and EMT's on the other side of the divided highway. The truck was in full sight thanks to the moon's light, and it was in bad shape. The police tape and the coroner's van told me that there were no survivors. Why did I feel bad? They were trying to kill us I reminded my subconscious. That didn't work as more and more guilt crept up and into my heart.

"Chystle's a killer..."

I don't know why I felt the need to say it out loud. She wasn't a murderer, as whoever was in the truck was trying to kill us. Those shots she took at the truck, she knew what she was doing. And what I was driving by now was the aftermath of her choice. I slowed down; a few other cars had to so it wasn't suspicious. I watched as a man loaded up a body bag into the van. I should've been more freaked out by this; Death was doing his work as I watched.

A feeling I'd never felt before began to stir inside of me. I couldn't explain it. I forced myself to break away from the slow motion I found myself in to get as far away from this scene as possible. I didn't like what I felt. It was a mixture of satisfaction and curiosity.

It felt morbid.
But it also felt right.

12

Blue Sky

State laws established as safeguards for investors against securities fraud.

First, phone calls that wake me up and now door bells. Hell, I was still in a fog over what happened late last night and into the early morning with Chrystle, so I wasn't even sure what I was going to do when I opened the door. Lo and behold, Amy was standing there, a smile so wide it may have had its own zip code.

"I know it's your day off, Kyle, but the office is closed for some reason or another and I needed to share this great news with someone!"

Her excitement was very much overwhelming as I was still pretty much asleep. "What's going on?" I mumbled.

"We did it. The state approved us to introduce even more RedKoin into the market. We can now even offer options contracts through their clearing corporation!" she practically yelled.

This was huge. In case you'd forgotten, options contracts were basically gambling instruments that allowed buyers and sellers to guess on what the future price of a security would be. Cryptocurrency wasn't defined as a security and as such, wasn't offered in contracts like this. Until now, apparently.

"We'll be offered on the same options boards as the euro dollar, the pound, and pretty much every other currency out there. Kyle, do you know what this means?" Amy asked.

"GenX is about to be very rich."

"Correction - we're about to be very rich. Do you think you can update the website to announce this news? I already have an approved communication we can use, signed off by the fed."

She handed me the typed-out memo, ready to be published.

The excitement of this development pushed everything else that had happened temporarily to the back of my mind. My mind fresh and anew with the idea of making more cash than I'd ever seen in my life propelled me back to the bedroom to grab my laptop. Amy was already making herself at home when I got back. I was up and running within the minute, the webpage editor ready to go with this amazing news.

The moment I hit the publish button, making the changes live, it felt like we needed to celebrate. "I know it's early, but I have some orange juice and champagne. A mimosa?" I asked.

"I think that's a wonderful idea."

As I made my way into the kitchen, everything from the night before came rushing back. If I asked why Amy had an FBI ID card in her possession, I'd not only be outing Chrystle but myself. No, that wouldn't do. Wait, what was I thinking? I wasn't getting involved in this until there was hard proof. Why did I have to keep reminding myself of that? It was like something deep down inside me wanted to pry more, find out what Amy truly knew.

When I came back out into the front room with the drinks, Amy had taken off her blazer and was lounging against the couch. There was something afoot here. "This reminds me of one of my favorite stories. Care if I share it with you?"

"Not at all."

"A long time ago, the Goddess of Love and Beauty was put on trial by her loved ones. Everyone had shunned her, including her family and the one she trusted the most. Just when it seemed as if she would die alone, one intervened - the God of Wealth and of Passings. He stood up to the one who would rather kill, telling them this was unjust and how dare they blame her for the fall. No one had anticipated that, for this particular god was seen as selfish and distant. However, that day, he fought tooth and nail to save the goddess from an untimely death, ultimately falling, but also proving himself to be an ally and the only person truly worth fighting for."

I didn't understand how that fit in. "That's an awesome story, but I'm not sure how exactly it fits in with what we're doing."

"In this case, I'm the one who was shunned by her family, never given a chance to succeed. Even with all of my successes, no one truly believed in me. That is, until I found you. With your skills and know-how, you are exactly the one I want to stand beside as this empire grows. Don't you feel it, too? Isn't there something stirring that you can't explain?"

"I-I don't know." This had gotten very intense, very fast.

"Ha-I mean Kyle. Sorry, my allergies are a little bad today. Why don't we continue this conversation later? Say, maybe a late dinner around nine-thirty?"

I had my previous engagement with Chrystle early, but all things considered... "Yeah, that'd be nice."

"Is it okay to assume this is a date? Are you okay with going on a date with your boss?"

A date? After my previous night with Chrystle, I didn't know about that. When she saw me hesitate, Amy spoke up. "There's one of two things happening here. You either have a girlfriend or you don't want to get yourself in trouble, legally."

"The second one never crossed my mind, actually," I admitted truthfully.

"I'm sorry, Kyle. I didn't know you were dating someone."

Technically, I wasn't. "We're not dating. To be honest, I don't even know where it stands."

"So, it's just a fling?"

"I have no idea what's going on. We're very different people and I don't even know that much about her."

Amy shook her head in understanding. "The allure of the unknown. I myself have been a victim of that."

"Do tell," I prodded.

"Please don't think poorly of me with this. I was once married, when I was too young and dumb to make the right choices. My husband was quite a bit older than myself, really just marrying me to hopefully take advantage of my growing fortune."

"You don't look old enough to have a story start this way."

She laughed at my comment and continued. "Thank you, Kyle. Either way, it was not a marriage made from love, rather opportunity. And much like opportunity, along came a man who presented much more of what I thought I wanted. I fell into his temptations, the great unknown as we just called it. It was only later that I realized he was a coward and an ass. By then, it was too late and the damage was done."

"I take it you're no longer married to the other guy?"

"His name was Hess, and no, we're not. Not long after our marriage was dissolved, he went back to Greece, where his family was from. I've not heard from him since."

"I'm sorry to hear that," I said.

"No, it was a valuable lesson. Be careful who you trust and remember, not everyone is who they seem to be."

The conversation moved onto other topics, but not for much longer. Amy eventually had other appointments to make and I needed to start getting ready for my latest caper with Chrystle. As she left, she grabbed my phone and put an address in my maps app. It was to a pretty exclusive Italian restaurant. We hugged and she went about her day, leaving me to my thoughts.

My main thought revolved around the story she told, how she succumbed to the unknown only to get hurt. It was ironic how she'd come to my apartment today, of all days, and for me to hear that particular story. Maybe someone above was watching over me.

How I wanted to proceed with Chrystle was the dominant topic the rest of the morning and into the early afternoon. I'd already showered, shaved, and was getting dressed when my second visitor arrived. This one was planned, but she was very early.

Even in khaki pants and a blue button down, Chrystle was a sight for sore eyes. I almost went for something more than a hug when a warning in my brain began to sound off. Instead, I gave her just a hug and got out of the way to let her in.

"That was a long night," she said, still yawning. "If I hadn't already said 'yes' to this crazy scheme, I'd still be sleeping."

"Speaking of which, I decided you'd need some protection for this. I hope this is okay."

She handed me something wrapped up in a cloth. I unwrapped it to reveal what looked to be a glass knife. "Never saw a knife made of glass before."

"That knife will get through any metal detectors that Director Herbert has. As noted, it's made of glass with a powder coating of clear ceramic. It won't break and it's just as sharp."

"Where do I put this thing?"

Chrystle had a second surprise. "Slip it into this moleskin pouch. This should fit comfortably on your belt and we can tuck it in, under your shirt. Trust me, I've done a lot of this covert stuff."

"This is what my tax dollars go towards, huh?" Chrystle wasn't expecting that snarky of a response. "I am kidding, but I do think taxation is theft. Just saying."

"Let's not bring politics into this."

"Fair point."

As a woman of her word, she helped me conceal the knife in such a way that it was comfortable for me and wouldn't be seen. I felt like a badass afterwards, ready to rumble at the first sight of danger. Actually, who was I kidding? I'd let Chrystle handle the problems and only step in if she told me to or it looked like she needed my help.

She was the badass here.

"We still have time. I wasn't expecting you here for another hour or so."

"I thought maybe we should talk about last night into the morning. Before we enter the snake pit, I wanted to make sure we were on the same page."

Oh boy.

I didn't really have an answer. I wasn't sure if she was talking about the rescue mission or the night we spent together on the uncomfortable cot. I assumed it was the first one and went that route to start. "Listen, I'm not dumb. I understand that there are certain aspects of your job that aren't pleasant. When I saw the dead bodies when I was driving home, it freaked me out a bit. I don't know that I could have done that."

"I was actually talking about our little adventure afterwards, but the fact that you're more concerned about the other details of my job is rather cute," she chuckled.

"Believe it or not, that was the most normal part of the night."

"We're good? You're not questioning your decision to get involved with this crusade?" Chrystle asked, her eyes laser focused on me as if I might try to run away, or something.

"Of course not," I responded. "I'll just be glad when the truth is uncovered and I can get back to a normal life."

She straightened my collar up for me. "What does a normal life look like for you, Kyle?"

"Going to work until five, five-thirty, coming home to someone. I can't actually see myself ever getting married or having kids, but I guess you shouldn't ever say never."

"That sounds like the dream, doesn't it?" she asked.

"What about you?" I turned it around on her.

"DARK will ensure my life is never normal, per se, but I'd like the things you mentioned. Most of the time, when I'm not on assignment, my schedule is a nine to five day. But, when duty calls," Chrystle finished.

"At least you'll never get bored," I countered.

"No, that's for sure. But, one of these days the job might catch up to me, like it did with Schulte and Muldoon."

God above, I hadn't even considered that.

The idea of death didn't necessarily scare me, but the idea of losing someone I cared about, potentially loved, that frightened me. Combined with what Amy had said before, maybe a relationship with Chrystle after this whole thing ended wasn't realistic.

"Look at the time," Chrystle said, quickly. "We'd better get going."

I knew we were still way early for the investors' event, but I was pretty sure I'd hurt Chrystle's feelings. I didn't take this as a good sign of things to come.

13

Treasury Bonds

A government bond issued by the US Treasury; usually with a life of thirty years

"Treasury bonds are the way to go if you want to finance long term with little risk," Kyle said, gushing out all of his investment knowledge on one of the FBI agents assigned to oversee our event.

I knew he was in good hands while I worked the room, trying to figure out what would be in our path to get the scythe Kronos asked for. As I walked around the far side of the ballroom in the Roosevelt building, I felt a hand grab me and pull me into the shadows. "Does he suspect anything, Chrystle?"

Standing beside me was Amy Pandemos. Much like me, she was wearing slacks and a blouse; much more unassuming than normal. "No, Mistress Aphrodite, he is still blissfully unaware."

"Good. Lord Hades' triumphant return needs to go off without a hitch. You've played your part so well in all of this. You shall be rewarded."

To hear Aphrodite tell me how pleased she was with my work inspired me. Not long after my introduction into DARK, she came to me as Venus Typhon. She introduced me to the true wonders of the world and to the man who would change this world forever, Lord Hades. When she told me of her plans, of how to first bring this world wealth and then to save it from a pandemic, I thought it was a bit far-fetched. However, as we were reaching the end of her plans and everything had fallen into place, I hated myself for doubting her.

"The last piece to the puzzle is getting Kyle to Kronos. Once there, the old Titan's aura will break the curse and Hades will be amongst us again," Aphrodite went over.

"And with his rise, we can finish the Hades Pathogen and unlock the Aphrodite Paradox."

She stroked my cheek with joy. "You have been such a loyal disciple. The way you hid all of Schulte's files and played your part well with not only Agent Muldoon, but with Agent Woodfield, have bought us the time we needed. Woodfield reported what happened to his director and in turn, collaborated your story with Herbert. They are suspicious of Amy Pandemos, a young businesswoman, and not a highly skilled agent in their midst."

"Wish me luck. Kronos would only meet us if we had his scythe in hand."

Aphrodite looked disgusted. "Giving such a powerful weapon to that traitor, it is a dangerous game."

"What if it were a replica?" I asked.

"He'd know and kill you."

"There has to be another way, Mistress."

She thought about it for a moment. "Doesn't this facility also have a few Stygian iron weapons hidden below?"

Stygian iron was a material that was said to have been forged in the River Styx, the only waterway in Hades' realm. While it was true that DARK had found a few of these over the years, they were locked away even more secure than the scythe. The only reason Kronos's scythe wasn't locked away even deeper was because Herbert had no idea what he had in his possession.

"I'm good, but even I can't get into that vault."

The Roosevelt Building where the event was being staged was also home to DARK's security vaults. The one Kyle and I needed to break into was on the second level. It would be hard to get into, not impossible though. The Stygian iron weapons were in the lowest vault, floor four. The only way to gain access to that was with Herbert's ID card and a copy of his fingerprint. Those were two things I knew I wouldn't be able to get on such short notice.

But Aphrodite might be able to.

"Herbert has a weakness for young women," I whispered. "Using your feminine wiles, you might be able to get into the vault while Kyle and I get Krono's scythe."

A cocky smirk grew on her face. "Yes – yes, this could work well in our favor. If successful, the weapon will be lying on the ground by your car. If you don't see it when you leave, assume I failed and go to Kronos. Turning Kyle into Hades is worth the cost, if we have to pay."

With a plan in place, I walked back out of the shadows, to find Kyle.

Soon Lord Hades, I told myself. I will free you from your prison and you will rise again.

****

"There you are, Kyle," I said as I walked over to where I left him.

"Sorry," he chuckled. "We got carried away talking about a retirement plan, didn't we, Bailey?"

I didn't know much about Agent Bailey, but the older man seemed to have truly been interested in what Kyle had told him. "Who knew that I was so far behind planning wise," the agent agreed.

"If it's okay with you, Agent Bailey, I'm going to take Kyle with me and introduce him to a few other people."

"By all means," he said. "Kyle, it was good talking to you."

"You, too, Ryan."

As we walked away, "Made a friend, huh?"

"That guy's had quite the career," Kyle said excitedly. "Though he was feeding me some fish story about a man-eating shark in the Mississippi. I think we'd have all heard about that one."

"Some cases stay classified for a very long time."

We had made it to the elevator. I waved at Doctor Jameson who was keeping Herbert's attention with some sort of graph. Good; keep him busy, please. I tried my best to hide my intentions and hit the down button. Jameson looked away as the doors opened and Kyle and I got in. As soon as they shut, I hit the button for the basement, level two. Kyle was fidgeting in the corner, looking about as uncomfortable as I felt concealing the truth from him. Lady Aphrodite had a plan and it was working perfectly. Even though I wanted nothing more than to tell him that he was the all-powerful Greek god of death, it wasn't my place to.

My feelings for Lord Hades, both before I met his incarnation as Kyle and after, couldn't cloud my judgment. Aphrodite and I had come too far for emotions to get in the way.

When the doors opened, it was go time. Immediately, one of the private security guards walked over to see who'd come down. "I'm sorry, but this area is-"

A perfectly placed punch to the weak jawline finished the sentence. "Restricted, I know."

"Holy crap! That was a perfect punch," Kyle whispered excitedly.

"That was just the beginning. Let's stay focused and not dawdle."

The basement, level two was pretty much a maze of long hallways and doors. My keycard granted us safety into most doors whenever a guard came around the corner. "How much farther?" Kyle asked as we snuck into another vault containing more trophies from the past.

“On the next turn, we’ll reach our destination. Be warned, there are no doors for us to sneak into in the hallway until the very end when we get to the storage unit that the scythe is in. If anyone catches us,” she warned, “we’ll need to be prepared for a fight.”

I could see his brain working a million miles a minute. If only he knew who he was. “Okay, we’re this far.”

As soon as the footsteps were out of range, I opened the door and we moved down and around. There it was, the red door that held the artifact we needed. I nudged Kyle forward and he followed me as I click clacked down the hall as fast as I could in four-inch heels. We were almost there when, “Freeze!”

Neither one of us turned around. I made eye contact with Kyle, hoping he understood that he was only to stay put. His eyes never left mine and he gave the slightest of nods. With that understanding established, I slowly turned around to see two of the security guards standing there. Neither had their sidearm out, which would prove to be a big mistake. Both were focused entirely on me, as well.

“I’m Special Agent Chrystle Marron, what seems to be the problem?”

“No one, on Director Herbert’s orders, is allowed in that vault. Keep your hands where we can see them and no one will have any issues," the smaller of the two men stated.

"You know who I am, an official member of the Department of Arcane Research and Knowledge. I want to know who you two are," I demanded.

The bigger guy looked a bit nervous. I'm sure they weren't used to actually dealing with anyone outside of Parkers or Lattrell. "We are Biggs and Wedge, two senior members of the private security firm Herbert hired."

Again, it was the small guy doing the talking.

All the bigger guy could do was look at his hands and twitch around. The expression, the bigger they are, the harder they fall came into my head and I couldn't quite hide my chuckle. For some reason, that unnerved the two of them even more.

I began walking towards them, keeping their attention on talking and not what actions I was about to commit. "Why is this the first time I'm seeing you two if you are senior members? You should know who I am if you are who you say you are."

"We know exactly who you are Agent Ma-"

It was in that moment I went low and swept the feet out of the smaller guard. As he fell, I disarmed the bigger guard, and slammed the butt of his gun into his knee. With both men on the ground, I pistol whipped them across their jaws, knocking them cold. With that taken care of, I placed the gun in my waistband and walked over to the door.

"Let's get this scythe and get out of here."

"You are such a badass," he said in awe.

"Thanks. I bet you have a bit of badass in you, too. We just need to unlock it."

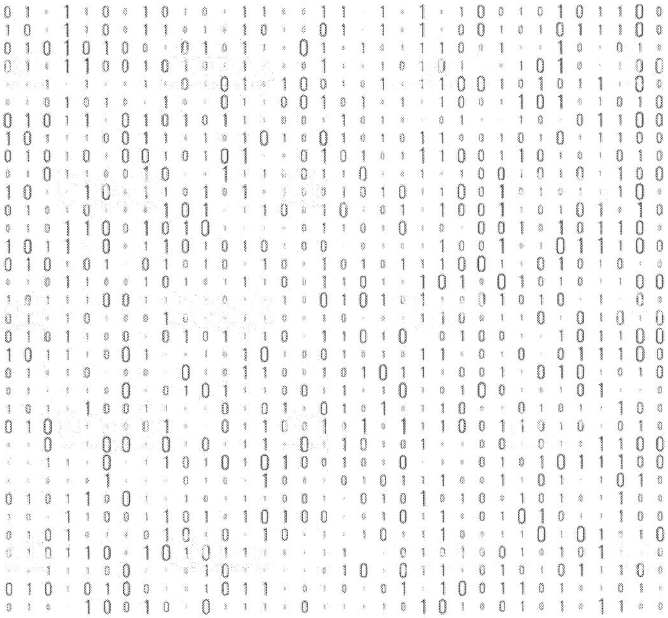

14

IPO

A type of public offering in which shares of a company are sold to institutional investors and usually also retail investors.

"What's that?" I asked Chrystle.

She bent down and picked up a short sword that appeared to be made out of a black iron-like material. "Who knows, but we should take it with us."

We had somehow swiped the scythe Kronos asked for and made it out with no one being none the wiser. Chrystle popped open the trunk and stashed the scythe and the sword back there. She removed the gun from her pants' waistband and handed it to me. "Place that in the glove box when you get in."

I did as instructed the moment I slid into the passenger seat. We were finally doing this. We were going to get to Kronos and find out if this USB really had incriminating evidence against Amy or prove once and for all that she ran a legit business. God, I was willing to jump through a bunch of hoops just to prove someone's innocence. Part of me missed the simpler times at Global Options, hanging out with Jeremiah and A.B. Though, this was sort of Jeremiah's fault with his dumb conspiracy theories and everything. Would Amy Pandemos even have found me if I hadn't done so much internet deep diving into her companies?

"The gang Kronos is a member of, the Titans, holes up in a bar called The Rings of Saturn. It's what you'd expect it to be, a biker bar with a lot of angry bikers," she explained.

I ran my hand through my hair. "I'm going to be bald at the end of this," I lamented.

"You'll be fine. Stay close and follow my lead, just like before."

When we got to the bar, there were only four motorcycles outside. I knew it was only a little after five in the evening, but I expected more. We exited the car, heading towards the trunk. "I'll carry the scythe in. If it's okay with you, can you hold onto the sword, just in case."

She had a gun, so I wasn't entirely sure why I needed a sword, but nothing about this situation was normal. As my hand closed around the sword's handle, I thought for a second I could hear faint whispering, like a voice that was really far off was trying to talk to me. After a moment, I realized I was probably just a bit nervous about going into a biker bar and shrugged it off to heightened emotions.

When we entered, there were four men sitting at a table in the center of the room. No one else was here and, more surprising, no beer at the table. The man in the middle looked younger than the three standing around him. He had an ugly scar that went down the side of his face, along with short, cropped blonde hair. He stood up as soon as he saw us and snapped his fingers. The three other men went around the bar and into a backroom.

"You must be Chrystle Marron."

"And you must be the hacker, Kronos."

He gestured for us to take a seat at his table. “The USB drive, please?” he asked as soon as we were seated.

Chrystle handed it over and he placed it into a small tablet that he produced from inside his leather jacket. He flipped out the small keyboard and began typing away. It didn’t take long for him to get what he was looking for. “Your boss knows that this can’t be undone, correct?”

“She does,” Chrystle answered.

She? I thought her boss had been Director Herbert? I didn’t even have time to ask what Kronos was talking about when he turned the screen towards me. There was no incriminating evidence towards Amy Pandemos, only binary code. The more I stared at it, the more hypnotized I became until the walls blocking long, forgotten memories exploded, drowning me in the past…

****

“Aphrodite, I find you guilty of all crimes brought against you.”

I was still me, but I wasn’t. I wasn’t just Kyle anymore, I was Hades, ruler of the Underworld. My brother, Zeus, was handing down some ridiculous sentence to Aphrodite and I just couldn’t stand by and watch his outrageous behavior anymore.

"This is a complete farce," I said, interrupting what I'm sure was a well-rehearsed speech he was giving to the rest of the Olympians. "Aphrodite's *crimes* as you call them wouldn't even be near the top of the worst deeds you've done today, let alone in your lifetime."

That had done it. "Hades, you have picked the wrong time to go on a moral crusade."

"I know who I am, Zeus and I don't pretend otherwise. You, on the other hand, are a blowhard and a tyrant."

"Silence!" Zeus bellowed. "I have had enough of you." He pulled out his lightning bolt and threw it right at Aphrodite, vaporizing the goddess on trial. "I hope you enjoyed the show."

That memory faded, turning into a new one.

This time, I was standing over my brother, both of us beaten and bloodied. "I hope you are happy with yourself, Hades."

"You brought this upon yourself when you killed Aphrodite in cold blood. Now, I have brought about the end of the gods. Without you, the rest will fall rather easily. It's time to let the humans screw up on their own and without your help," I said, coughing up a little blood.

"You're going to die, too."

"Funny enough, I do believe I am exempt from your fate. What that entails, I do not know, but I do know this. I won't see you in the afterlife this time."

As I jabbed my Stygian iron sword into his heart, Zeus jammed his lightning bolt into my stomach, ending my time as Lord of the Dead…

For now.

****

"Kyle, are you okay?"

"I don't think that's the human anymore."

I opened my eyes and saw Chrystle and Kronos both looking towards me from their seats. "I don't think we need to play games anymore."

Kronos clapped his hands together. "Hades lives again."

"How in the name of the Fates did you escape Zeus, Kronos?" I asked.

"Me and my brethren knew the time of the gods and the Titans was over. We adapted better, stayed hidden," he answered.

Chrystle bowed her head to me. "And do you know my secret, Lord Hades?"

"You can still call me Kyle and yes, I know. You're a follower of Aphrodite, the goddess who somehow survived Zeus' lightning bolt. I have quite a few questions for her."

Kronos stood up. "I delivered what she asked. Where is my payment?"

Thousands of years of bad memories informed me that there was no way I was letting Kronos get his scythe back. If Zeus was awful, Kronos, at full power, was a world killer. "Did you think I would let you take your scythe back without protest?" I asked.

"I freed you from your prison, Hades. You owe me."

"I owe you nothing."

He kicked the table, sending both Chrystle and me tumbling backward. He grabbed his scythe, but not before I was back on my feet. I heard a commotion coming from the backroom where his brothers Atlas, Hyperion, and Krius were. "Chrystle, get that door locked. I'll take care of Kronos."

The Titan twirled his scythe around lovingly. "We are both shadows of our former selves, but that doesn't mean this will be anything less than a good old-fashioned brawl."

"I once killed Zeus. I can end you, too."

Three gunshots broke up the intense stare down. Chrystle had opened the door and fired upon the other three Titans. They were lying down in a pile. "I doubt they are dead, but they won't be interfering."

Kronos looked rather pissed and swung the scythe at me with his full fury. I blocked his blow with the Stygian iron sword that had to have been a gift from Aphrodite. With his flank exposed, I punched him in the side of the head. If an ass whipping was what he wanted, then I was more than happy to oblige.

Kronos spit out a bit of blood and returned to his fighting stance. “Here I was worried you’d be out of practice.”

“I was worried you’d take it easy on me, old man.”

“Who the hell are you calling old, Hades?”

The two of us charged each other again, this time we tossed our weapons aside. We were going to decide this the right way, with our fists. He connected first, his hard knuckles digging into my rib cage. I pushed through the pain and returned the favor smack dab on his nose. That didn’t even budge Kronos as he kneed me in the gut. Even with my wind knocked out of me, I followed up with an elbow to the back of his neck.

Once that short sequence was finished, both of us dropped to a knee.

“Damnit, Hades. Just let me have my scythe and go.”

“So, you can do what? Destroy the world, Kronos? I killed Zeus to make sure that didn’t happen.”

He actually had the nerve to start laughing at me, like it was all some sort of joke. “Look around,

Hades! We have no power anymore. I ain't destroying this world! But I'll tell you who will."

Chrystle closed ranks as Kronos picked himself off, wiping away more blood that was streaming from his nose. "What are you talking about, Titan?" she asked.

"Aphrodite - she's going to be the one to end this world if she's allowed to finish that Hades Pathogen she's been working on," Kronos explained.

"How do you know about that?" Chrystle questioned.

"Girl, I am older than time itself. I didn't stay alive this long by being in the dark when others are scheming."

I remembered that name from when Amy, errr, Aphrodite showed me around GenX. "She told me that project was to find a vaccine that would be used for multiple viruses."

"Viruses she's been creating, Hades. Use that damn head of yours to see what's actually going on."

"Why are you revealing yourself to us now, Kronos? I've been tracking you for years and you've never let me get this close?"

"Because Agent Marron, even though you're her lackey, I think deep down you're also a smart lady," he said. "If you two don't stop Aphrodite from unleashing Hell on Earth, there won't be anyone left to worship her."

"She hopes that if she is worshipped again, that her powers will return?"

"The way she died, some of her powers never left. But for old ones like us, they're probably not coming back at all."

"She told me Hades would regain his power, that together, the three of us would be able to correct this world," Chrystle lamented.

"She lied to you. Aphrodite's got a soft spot for this one after he defied Zeus and probably hopes his powers will come back, but I'm telling you both, it ain't happening."

The way Kronos said it, the way he was so sure of his belief made me feel the same way. He must've known this from trying to get his former glory back and failing numerous times. That's when I made my mind up. I walked over and picked up his scythe. "If you try anything, so help me, I will come back."

Kronos reached out and took it from me, slowly. "I just want to be whole again. If I'm cursed to live life basically as a mortal, I, at least want to have something from my past to hold onto."

"Don't make me regret this decision, Kronos. Now if you'll excuse us," I laced my arm through Chrystle's, "we need to meet with Aphrodite and straighten a few things out."

"Be careful - if you're not with her, she'll turn on you."

"Thanks for the advice," I shot back.

"This ain't going to be like dealing with Zeus, boy," he kept on going. "That old son of a bitch had one goal in mind. No, you're dealing with a woman scorned who liked to keep secrets from everyone."

"Anything else you want to tell me, doctor?"

"Just don't turn your back on an enemy."

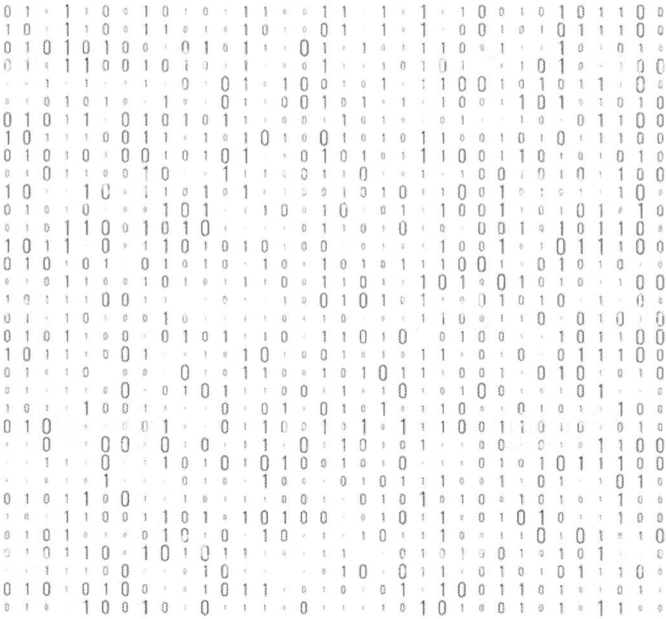

15

Expiration

The last date on which the holder of the option may exercise it according to its terms.

We were back where it all began, War Dog Labs. Chrystle had set this up, telling Aphrodite that we needed to see her at the abandoned building as soon as possible. Something had come up during our encounter with Kronos and it couldn't wait to be dealt with. The moment we turned into the parking lot, Aphrodite was standing there. The smile she was wearing on her face as she saw me, Hades and not Kyle, lit up the night sky.

"Are you two okay?" she asked immediately as we got out of the car.

"Yeah, we're fine, Aphrodite. However, Kronos brought up some issues that I think the two of us need to discuss."

"Hades, why on Earth would you listen to what Kronos says?"

"Mistress, some of the allegations he brought up were quite horrible," Chrystle added.

"Do tell…" she responded, her voice becoming guarded.

That's when I unloaded everything. She stood there as I ranted about her crazy idea to unleash some killer virus in my name, only to then bring about a vaccine to whoever remained from the nightmare. I questioned how someone could think it was worth it to basically become a serial killer, all in the hopes that they regained their powers if they were seen and worshipped as a hero. I finished my soapbox speech with a question. "I killed Zeus because of his lunacy; why would you want to go down the same road as your attempted murderer?"

"Because I'm different from Zeus, Hades."

I wanted to believe her, but I knew greed when I saw it. She had the same expression Zeus did the day of the trial and when I killed him. "Do you really believe that?" I asked.

"Hades, why are you questioning me?"

"I can't let you do this." I took a step closer. "You were once so full of love and acceptance. Don't let your past, the actions of a dead man, influence you today."

"If you aren't with me, you are against me."

A chill went down my spine as she said it. This was the exact warning Kronos had given me before we left his bar. "You tried to enlist Kronos in this gambit before, haven't you?"

"And you killed Ares when he turned you down, too."

"Chrystle, what are you talking about?" I asked.

"Agent Muldoon and I found a man chained up and close to death in War Dog Labs when we investigated it after the fact," she told me. "I didn't know who he was until later, when I told Aphrodite what I witnessed. Ares died because he refused to help you."

That's when the goddess began to clap. "This was the long game, yes, but the end goal was always to bring Hades back. When neither Kronos nor Ares could be of help, I discarded them. I don't regret my decisions."

"What do you need from me anyways for this killer virus?"

"Your blood unlocks both the pathogen and the cure. Don't you see?" she went on. "Once we save the world from this virus, we will be treated as gods once again and I'll regain my true form."

"I don't see why you need to."

"What did you say, Hades?"

"You're beautiful, as a person and how you treated me. I never cared about your outer beauty, like the others did," I told her, honestly. "Is Agent Schulte a willing host for you?"

It was Aphrodite's turn to drop her tough woman act. "No, she is not."

"Mistress, I'd be a willing host, if we could co-exist in harmony," Chrystle offered.

"Give this up, let's live life, normally."

****

I was in the middle of cleaning out my desk at GenX. With Agent Rebecca Schulte freed from Aphrodite's control, that meant we had to stage the death of Amy Pandemos. Thankfully Agent Schulte had no memories of her time as Aphrodite's host and wasn't able to throw any kinks into the story that Chrystle and I told local authorities.

Amy Pandemos had committed suicide.

Of course, with that came the reorganization of GenX and Ares Commerce.

The last worry I had was the fact that Amy was just a glamored version of Rebecca. When I brought that up, Chrystle (with whom Aphrodite had merged with) eased my concerns. "Remember, you were reborn as Kyle, that's why everyone can see you, knows who you are. When Aphrodite took over Agent Schulte's form, her godly essence dressed it up a bit. I promise, no one will figure it out."

Just because I was the Greek God of Death didn't mean I'd be cool with going to jail. Still, since Amy had just hired me before her *big demise*, I was the first casualty of the board of directors' new vision of the companies. Which led me to my first call when I got to my car. "Jeremiah! How are you, man?"

"I'm guessing you are looking for a job after what I read in the papers?" he asked.

"Yep."

"Hell man, we still have plenty of room. See you Monday."

And just like that, I had my old job back. Things were starting to feel normal again. Or as normal as they could after coming to terms with everything that had happened. In the spirit of being, I turned on some classic tunes, rolled the windows down, and rocked out all the way home. I ever threw the aviator sunglasses on to complete the look.

Just as things were looking up, I had a bad feeling sink the fun out of me as soon as I pulled into my apartment complex. Outside my unit were four motorcycles - the Titans were here. I reached into the back seat and pulled out the Stygian iron sword I'd kept, just in case. It seemed like that was a warranted decision. As I walked by the bikes, I slashed the tires, ensuring these scumbags weren't going anywhere. That's when I heard a gunshot.

I stormed into the apartment to see one of the brothers lying on his back with a hole in his head. I immediately knew this Titan was dead, my lingering intuition confirming that with no hesitation. The two others were flanking Kronos who was trying to beat down the bedroom door. "I know you are in there, Aphrodite. I will kill you!"

I rushed forward and stabbed the closest Titan to me through the back. He fell, joining his other dead brother in whatever horrible afterlife was awaiting them. I followed up with a backhand slice that removed the head of the third brother. Only Kronos remained, his scythe reflecting the murderous look he was casting my direction.

"How dare you come into my house with murderous intentions!"

"You talk to me like I'm the villain? You're the one keeping the wench alive who would wipe out this planet."

The door flew open and Chrystle (or maybe Aphrodite was in control now) was pointing her gun at Kronos.

"Hades showed you mercy the other night and this is how you repay him?"

"Aphrodite - once you are dead, all the sins you committed against me will be avenged. Hades, don't get involved again," he warned me.

"You're in my house; you don't get to make the rules."

Kronos reached back with scythe, his intent clear. Aphrodite, controlling Chrystle pointed her gun at the attacking Titan at the same time I thrusted forward with my blade. The shot pushed him back, onto the Stygian iron, killing him instantaneously. I let go of the sword and moved to embrace the shaken goddess. She nestled her head into my shoulder, shaking over the situation that just happened.

"Never turn your back on an enemy," I reminded her.

"I've never felt so vulnerable. How do we do this, Hades?" Aphrodite asked.

"We're no longer all powerful; we can't control what happens next. That's when you can truly begin living."

"You don't have to share headspace with anyone else," she admitted. "This is hard, Hades."

"It won't be. And I'm Kyle; Hades for all intent and purpose is long gone. The memories might remain, but I haven't been a god in millennia."

Her eyes flashed a golden yellow before returning to Chrystle's natural green. "I'm not going to sugarcoat it, it's weird having her as a part of me."

"Do you regret it?"

"Not at all, Kyle. In fact, when I get back to DARK, her knowledge is going to be very helpful moving forward with an agenda - after I get rid of Director Herbert and his council of stooges."

I looked around at the mess and the dead bodies. Crap. "I guess we better call the police as I'm sure someone else around here already has."

"You're always welcome to crash at my place, if you want to."

"I just might take you up on that offer."

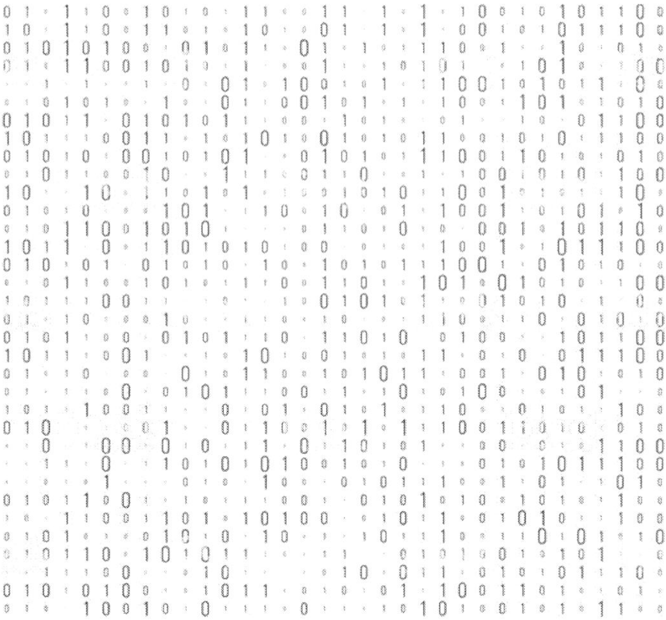

16

One Year Later...

"Sam, what's the good word," I said as I answered the phone.

"Kyle, let's buy five hundred more RedKoins and go ahead and liquidate GenX at the market price. Man, I held onto that one way too long," my favorite client moaned.

We still hadn't changed our policy about giving advice, even though I knew GenX was a dog after everything I'd been through. "Okay, orders placed," I confirmed with Sam. "Anything else I can do for you today?"

"You know what, let's take the deep dive and place some uncovered calls. I'm feeling lucky today, Kyle."

It felt good to just have an ordinary day and helping people with decisions, both good and bad. I was where I belonged, at Global Options as Kyle Carlisle. I wasn't Hades, I wasn't a god, I was just another guy who happened to have a rather long and complicated backstory. Hell, my girlfriend was a duel personality black ops agent with DARK, so I doubt you could expect much less.

It was actually through DARK where I could channel the little bit left of my former life. Aphrodite, through Chrystle, wasn't sure if we were truly immortal anymore. "We may have long lives ahead of us, but I do have a feeling this might be the last chapter we write."

"I'm okay with that," I remember telling her.

"Kyle," A.B. shouted, nearly causing me to jump out of my skin. "A few of us are going golfing, well actually drinking while on a golf course, but we're calling it golfing. Are you in?"

"Absolutely, my man. Chrystle actually bought me a set last week for my birthday. I haven't even gotten to test them out, yet."

"Dude, me and you, the driving range after work. I'll call your secret agent girlfriend myself and tell her," he snorted.

Most of the folks at Global Options assumed Chrystle worked for the FBI and that was fine by us. Speaking of the FBI, we'd kept tabs on Agent Schulte. She'd recently been promoted to senior agent for her work in financial crimes. I could neither confirm nor deny if she had an inside source who fed her information, off the books. She'd also ensured that Agent Drew Muldoon was paid the proper respects.

I think he was Aphrodite's biggest regret.

That'd be one we all have to live with, unfortunately.

"Don't worry about her. Chrystle's off on assignment in Cuba, I think. Some fishermen apparently found some sort of old nuclear weapons cache and the skeleton to an abnormally large shark. Don't ask me anything else, I don't know," I reminded him.

A.B. loved to get as much dirt as I could provide him when it came to covert missions. "Dude, nukes and a shark corpse? You gotta give me more than that!"

"Like I said, I don't know anything else. Been down at the bottom of the bay for a long time, the FBI imagines."

I may have intentionally left out the part about human bones found near the shark's, but these things slip my ancient mind.

"When she gets back, we're all going out for beers so I can hear about this."

My phone rang, forcing A.B. to give up his quest of getting information I didn't have. I looked at my caller ID and smiled. "Sam, two calls in ten minutes - what's going on?"

"So, is there any way possible to cancel those uncovered calls? My wife's about to kill me."

"Don't worry, Sam, you're my guy. Let's see what we can do."

And just like that, my life was right back to where it needed to be - normal.

FBI Case File DM-169172
(The Unredacted Version)

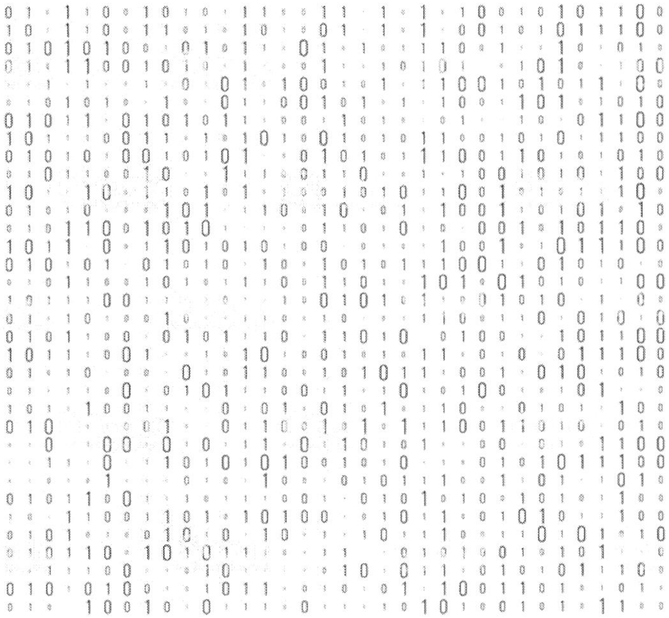

Prospectus

A formal document that is required by and filed with the federal regulators that provides details about an investment offering to the public.

Schulte dropped the case file on my desk. “Looks like we got a fun one, Muldoon.”

It was too early in the morning for this bullshit. “Take that file and shove it. I’m about to go on vacation.”

“No can do, my friend. This apparently takes priority over a four-day weekend.”

Ughhh, this was the third long weekend I'd lost this year. Annoyed, I opened the file and began to read what was so damn important. Some biotech firm, GenX, was claiming that a competitor had stolen proprietary information from them. While I thought most of the dossier was completely stupid and useless, my eyes grew wide at the very end. One of the projects that GenX claimed sensitive was information stolen from a vaccine. If a company was in the middle of developing a vaccine for something, that also meant they needed the virus that it would be used to combat.

"Are you thinking what I'm thinking, Schulte?" I asked.

"Are you thinking about the ramifications of blowing off an assignment?"

"No, I'm thinking biological weapon."

Schulte just shook her head. "This is about money, Muldoon. GenX had that flop when they went public, and now they're seeking retribution. Stop with your ridiculous conspiracy theories," she snorted.

Greed was an easy problem to solve. "Okay, so let's just go down to see whoever runs this operation - what's it called?" I asked before reading the answer myself, "War Dog Labs. Maybe we can clear this up, and I can head off into the mountains for a relaxing weekend."

“Yeah, let’s see how that goes,” she agreed.

With a plan in place, I grabbed the keys to our FBI issued ride and off to War Dog we went. No sooner did we get into the building did we meet resistance. “Who are you two?” a security guard asked immediately.

Schulte flashed her FBI badge. “I’m Agent Rebecca Schulte, and this is my partner, Agent Drew Muldoon.”

That got us escorted out of the building. “Sorry, no warrants, no entry,” the guard said happily.

Once back in the car, “There’s no way we’re getting a warrant without some sort of proof.”

“You’re right, Muldoon, but I think I see an opportunity.”

Schulte pointed to the other side of the parking lot. A man was yelling furiously at another guard near his car. The two of us casually walked over, into hearing distance. “You can’t fire me!” the man yelled. “You can tell Venus that I’ll expose her just like I did at GenX!”

The guard pushed the man towards his car and left without saying another word. As soon as he went back into the building, Schulte and I made our approach. “You okay?” she asked him.

Schulte was a much better good cop than I’d ever be.

The man appeared to be in his mid-forties, a bit pudgy, with ruffled black hair and coke bottle glasses. “Absolutely not. For the second time in months, I’ve been fired from a job over concerns about what’s going on inside.”

I flashed my ID. “I’m Agent Muldoon, and this is my partner, Agent Schulte. Do you mind if we ask you a few questions?”

“Feds… of course you’re feds.”

“That wasn’t a no,” I responded.

He patted the sweat away from his forehead. “My story needs alcohol to tell. Meet me at Jak D’s and buy me the first round, and you got yourself a deal.”

“Absolutely,” Schulte chimed in before I could say no.

“The name’s Nate Plopper. I’ll see you in ten.”

I gave Schulte the silent treatment until we turned out of War Dog Labs’ parking lot. “I could’ve just beaten the information out of that creep,” I snapped.

“Muldoon, we’re going for a more subtle touch.”

The two of us were about as opposite as could be. I was a late thirties white guy with some anger issues and no college education. Schulte was the youngest agent on the scene at twenty-four, an orphan from Hong Kong who was adopted here, and went on to become one of the smartest people

I'd ever have the pleasure of meeting. Rumors around the field office were the two of us were dating on the sly, but we'd never crossed that line.

Even if we had talked about it a time or two.

"This guy is just as dirty as everyone inside that joint," I countered with.

"Probably, but all we need is a bit of evidence, and ta-da, the warrant is ours."

I really hated it when she was right. I kept my mouth shut as I followed Plopper. Once we got to Jak D's, the chubby little guy wasted no time getting inside and pulling up to the bar. The moment we joined, Schulte held up three fingers and pointed to the tap. The bartender nodded and went to work. We just sat in silence, as it appeared Plopper wasn't going to talk until the beer was delivered.

The moment the glass was set down in front of him, "Okay, time to talk."

"Agent Muldoon, right?" he asked me.

"That's correct."

"Have you ever lost a job for being a whistleblower?"

"I have not," I answered.

"Is that what happened to you just now?" Schulte asked.

"God no, I was fired from War Dog Labs for something else. But my story starts at GenX." He took a big swig of his beer. "I'm a computer engineer by trade and my latest project from our mystery CEO was for me to start mining cryptocurrencies."

I just shrugged; this was Schulte's area of expertise so I backed down. "That doesn't seem like a very dark thing to do. In fact, it's a great way to make money, especially after their IPO failed, wouldn't you agree?"

"Between us, the failed IPO and the leaked information to War Dog Labs was an inside job. The reason I was instructed to lead the team to mine for cryptocurrency and the reason I was fired was one in the same," he said, breathing very heavily.

"What was it?" Schulte asked.

"GenX and War Dog Labs are run by aliens."

Son of a bitch.

I wasn't paying for this idiot's beer.

"Well, thank you for wasting our time," I grumbled.

"Another skeptic, but I tell you, GenX and by extension, War Dog Labs, are in on the conspiracy. It's all detailed on my blog, by the way."

I was giving Schulte the death stare and she took the hint. "Thanks for your time, Mister Plopper," she said politely.

"Yeah, thanks for nothing," I added.

****

"He was right; he detailed all his crazy theories right here on his website, Muldoon."

"Great, so our best lead is a giant nut job."

Schulte didn't even look up, quite obviously taking a ride down this rabbit hole. "He's a nut job, that's for sure, but I'm trying to find the truths that are hidden in the mess."

"What in God's name could you find in this mess?" I asked.

"He really rants and raves about the CEO of GenX. Apparently, no one is one hundred percent sure who owns it, but that's not the juiciest part," she went on.

"Don't keep me in suspense," I said, sarcastically.

She scrolled down to another post. "Plopper claims that the GenX leak was an inside job. He goes on to say that it wasn't enough to expose the aliens, of course, but I think he may have been onto something."

"What do you suggest we do?"

"Instead of banging on War Dog's door, we should go to GenX and see what we can dig up."

That wasn't a half bad suggestion. "It's a bit late tonight for that, but that sounds like a great plan for first thing in the morning."

I began to stretch out and call it a night. It was bad enough my extended weekend was ruined, but

I wasn't going to sleep here, either. I said my good evenings to Schulte and headed for the exit. I didn't even get to open the door before she came sprinting up to me.

She wasn't even breathing hard, which annoyed me for some reason. "Forget GenX for a moment, I think I found something on Plopper's site that gets us a meeting with Venus Typhon, the CEO of War Dog Labs."

"This better be good. You're cutting into my beer drinking time."

"Plopper uploaded proof that the CFO of War Dog Labs is laundering money. I'm sure everyone assumes Plopper's an idiot," she began.

"I know I do."

"And never bothered to look through all the noise. Maybe we take one more hit at War Dog before we seek a warrant."

I knew that look too well. Schulte had a plan. "What are you thinking we do? Barnstorm the building again and hope that she's still there and will talk to us?"

"I have a better idea."

Within five minutes of Schulte finding Typhon's number and speaking with her, we had a meeting set up for later tonight; nine thirty at War Dog Labs. "I can't believe you pulled that off," I admitted.

"I learned from the best."

I knew she was patronizing me and I just ignored it. "There's a chance this could be some sort of setup. Make sure you're stocked and loaded, please."

"Not everything we do ends up in a shootout, Muldoon."

"You said something similar before we got into a shootout with that cartel the other week," I reminded her. "To be on the safe side, can you see who's on call? Let's have two agents go pick up the money launderer and bring him in, just in case."

She did a quick search and saw that Agents Taft and Cleveland were the on-call guys. "Can you call them?" she asked.

"Why? Afraid to ruin anyone else's plans?"

"I didn't ruin them, the chief did," she reminded me.

"I'm sure you had nothing to do with it, either."

That didn't stop her from handing me her cell phone. "I'll owe you one."

I snatched it and made the call out. "Cleveland, it's Muldoon, can you and Taft grab a guy if I send you the information? Excellent, thanks for your help."

The moment I hung up, she snapped the phone right out of my hands. "You're a better bad cop than I am."

"We got two hours before we're supposed to meet Typhon. Let's go grab a cup of coffee and a slice of pie," I suggested.

****

I dug into my blackberry pie without hesitation. "Can't believe you ordered a fruit parfait," I said between bites. "What kinda un-American FBI agent are you?"

"This is why I can run without sounding like I'm dying."

Another forkful of pie entered my mouth. "At least I'll die happy."

Both of our phones immediately went off, interrupting our philosophical discussion of the merits of pie. "Damnit," I grumbled.

"What's the irony that we're getting a call about shots fired a block from War Dog Labs?"

"This is your fault." I tossed my fork onto my plate.

It didn't take long to get from the diner to where the call was reported. We were two streets over from War Dog and the moment we pulled in, we saw the gunmen slinking around the building. It was two guys in fancy suits, shooting at an unknown target two windows up from the parking lot. We got out with our weapons drawn. We used our car as cover.

"I think we can get the jump on them. They didn't even look over when we pulled in," I observed.

"They don't look like your normal shooters."

"My bullets don't discriminate. We'll give 'em a chance, but if they turn on us, shoot to kill."

We left the safety of the car as the two guys fired off a couple more shots towards the windows on the second floor again. I went first, with Schulte hot on my heels. As soon as we got into shooting range, we both pointed our sidearms at the men. "Stop, FBI!" I shouted.

Both guys turned towards me. They had weird looks in their eyes and their intent was clear. They were going to open fire on us. I never gave them a chance. I double tapped the trigger, putting both guys down before either could make a move.

"Let's go see what they were shooting at."

"Muldoon, are you okay?"

"Yeah, just something was off with those guys. We'll talk about it later."

The auspicious office building beside us now loomed over. I'm not sure why, but a chill ran down my back. Hurrying, we entered and took the stairwell to the left to the second floor. Once we got to our target destination, there was nothing. The whole floor was cleaned out, not a desk, table, chair on the floor. The only thing that told us something was wrong were the broken windows and the bullet holes in the ceiling. With absolutely nothing to go on here, we returned to the dead bodies below. I took one and Schulte took the other. My corpse had a War Dog Labs badge on his belt.

"This guy worked at War Dog, Jon Rowbick," I said.

"This guy over here not only worked at War Dog, he was the CFO - Matt Megan."

"The money launderer that we sent Taft and Cleveland to pick up?" I asked.

"The very same," she confirmed.

What the hell was going on? "When they turned in my direction, there was a weird look in their eyes. You ever see a feral dog, Schulte?" I asked.

Feral dogs were a rare sight on the streets, but I'd come across a few in my day. "No, but I've heard stories from my dad when I was a kid. Don't feed ferals or strays, he'd tell me. They'd rather bite the hand that feeds them than wait for more."

It felt like we were being played. "Get in the car - we're going to War Dog and getting answers, now."

Before I started the engine, both of us reloaded. Something in the pit of my stomach told me that our night was just beginning. No sooner did I turn out of the parking lot, another car came racing around the corner. It skidded too far to the right before adjusting itself and making a beeline straight for Schulte and me. I punched the gas and took off straight. Schulte rolled her window down and began firing. I tried to radio Cleveland and Taft, but got no answer from them.

I hoped to hell and back that they were okay.

I heard the very distinct sound of a tire blowing. "You get 'em?" I yelled over to my partner.

"I took out the front passenger tire, but they're still coming. Bought us some time, though."

Good.

I saw our spot; just ahead was a little league baseball field. I turned in and spun the car around. Getting it into park and grabbing my weapon, both of us were pointing our guns out the windows when the chasing car pulled in. It rolled to a complete stop about five feet from us.

There was no one in the driver's seat.

"None of this makes sense, Schulte."

"I'm starting to think Plopper wasn't a lunatic afterall."

"Someone is going to great lengths to keep us from War Dog Labs; that's what I'm taking from this," I tried to reason.

"Keep us from there or just delay our visit?" Schulte asked.

Either way, we knew exactly where we needed to go now. I shifted the car into drive and didn't stop until we entered the parking lot of War Dog. I idled the car at the very rear of the lot, not ready to park just yet. Both of us surveyed the scene - it was quiet. No other cars were in the lot and no lights were on inside. I drifted into a spot close to the building.

"There's a decent chance this is a setup, right?" Schulte asked me.

"The odds are in our favor of that."

"Was that a joke, Muldoon?"

"It happens every so often."

No sooner did we get out of the car, shots from the third floor began raining down on us. This night just wouldn't end.

"This is your fault, Rebecca."

"Using my first name, I must be in trouble now," she quipped.

"You have no idea."

Printed in Great Britain
by Amazon

63503366R00111